MIDNIGHT AT THE ELECTRIC

ALSO BY JODI LYNN ANDERSON

Tiger Lily

The Vanishing Season

Peaches

midnight at the electric

JODI LYNN ANDERSON

HarperTeen is an imprint of HarperCollins Publishers.

Midnight at the Electric
 For information address HarperCollins Children's Books, a division of HarperCollins Publishers, 195 Broadway, New York, NY 10007.
www.epicreads.com

Library of Congress Control Number: 2017932844
ISBN 978-0-06-239354-8

Typography by Sarah Nichole Kaufman
17 18 19 20 21 PC/LSCH 10 9 8 7 6 5 4 3 2 1
❖
First Edition

For Jamie

SWEETHEARTS SAT IN THE DARK AND SPARKED.

—Woody Guthrie,
"So Long, It's Been Good to Know Yuh (Dusty Old Dust),"
a Dust Bowl song

MIDNIGHT AT THE ELECTRIC

ADRI

PART 1

CHAPTER 1

From above, Miami looked as if it were blinking itself awake; the rising sun reflected against the city's windows. Adri—in fuzzy extra-large pajama pants, her messy black hair pulled back in a rubber band—had pulled over on the shoulder of the Miami bridge. Her Theta had blown a circuit board and she needed to fix it. Now, she took in the view one last time: it wasn't much, but she'd never see it again.

The sky lay low and gray over South Beach. The empty beachfront hotels lay dark, water halfway up their lowest windows. All along the waterfront, buildings stood stark and abandoned. Neighborhood by neighborhood, the ocean had crept into the city, making it look like a kingdom from an old fairy tale, like Atlantis disintegrating into myth. The morning's mail drones were already buzzing above the waterlogged buildings below, swaying in the heavy winds but staying on course to deliver packages to anyone who was left: the ruggedly independent, the people with nowhere else to go.

Adri had been one of them until today; her entire life had been spent watching the city get swallowed by water. She wouldn't miss it, but she had to take a deep breath as she turned back to the car. She gathered the papers and wrinkled sweatshirts that had fallen out when she'd stepped out onto the pavement and shoved them into the back. She carefully plucked a caterpillar off her windshield, sliding her fingers against it gently and moving it to the bridge rail. Then she started the car and set it to self-navigate. Her restless mind drifted to Kansas and what lay ahead. She opened her placement letter on the dash monitor and reread it.

Dear Ms. Ortiz,

We try to arrange homestays for our Colonists-in-Training as often as possible, to maintain a sense of normalcy at a deeply transitional time. We're delighted to inform you that we've located a distant cousin of yours (a Lily Vega, maiden name Ortiz, age 107) within driving distance of the Center, who is willing to welcome you into her home during the next three months. Please make your way to this address and await instructions.

268 Jericho Road
Canaan, KS 67124

Sincerely,
Lamont Bell
Director

Adri hadn't even known she'd had cousins, or any family, left alive. Her parents had been only children; she'd never known of anyone even remotely related to them.

She turned on the news, and when people honked at her to tell her Theta was trailing sparks (it often did) she casually gave them the finger. She leaned back in her seat to watch the sky through the big sunroof. She felt lighter the farther she got from the city.

The coast fell away, and with it, the flooded towns and cities. The ride was only twelve hours with the new interstate, and with a speed limit of a hundred and fifty, it flew by. Normally she would have taken the spare time to study, but all of her devices had been remotely disabled the day she'd received her acceptance letter. Colonists were supposed to spend their last three months focusing on what they learned at the Center in Wichita. Other than that, they were supposed to do as close to nothing as possible.

Only a week had passed since the message had flashed on her wristTab, releasing a spray of holographic balloons that spiraled up around her and away as her admission note flashed on the screen. It was a cheesy touch, but her heart had dropped to her feet anyway. It was the first time in her life she could remember crying. Everything she'd sacrificed and worked for since the sixth grade—the late nights studying, the relentless schedule of exercise, course work, and training—was going to pay off. Within months, she'd be one of the lucky few living on Mars.

The air turned colder the farther she rode. It was long past dark when she crossed the border into Kansas, and another hour before she exited the highway. Nearing Canaan, each turn seemed to take her farther and farther into the middle of nowhere, county roads unfurling darkly under a sky black as ink. The Theta began to make a loud, thumping sound. Around eleven, she switched the car to driver-navigate and steered it gingerly along. It was practically dead when she pulled up to the end of the driveway.

Adri gazed around; the place looked almost abandoned. There was a little white farmhouse with peeling siding and a small barn lot . . . leaning fences surrounding a large pasture, a bunkhouse (or was it a stable?) listing to one side. An ancient SUV sat in the driveway—one of the last of the great gas guzzlers.

Adri cut the power and blinked at a sign by the flowerbeds drying up for the winter. There were indications of life though: a series of purple plastic dragonflies lined the path to the front door and a tin angel with a watering can stood poised over a patch of daisies and weeds to her right. A little placard poking up by the path said: *Come in, my flowers would like to meet you.*

"Oh God," she muttered.

She took a deep breath.

She turned her attention upward. The sky was closer here than it had been back home, or at least it felt that way. *That's where I'll be*, she thought. *That's where I'm going.* In a way, she was already gone. That was what she needed to focus on.

She checked herself in the mirror. She looked like she'd just rolled out of bed, which was how she always looked. She brushed herself off and got out of the car, a few soda cans and empty wrappers trailing out with her feet.

A sign had been taped to the door, written in shaky handwriting.

> *Adri, I stayed up as late as I could, but I'm old! Your room is upstairs to the right. Can't wait to meet you. Don't let the bed bugs bite.* ☺☺☺

Adri moved through the house in the dark, bumping into corners and staring around into the shadowy rooms before she made her way up the stairs. One room stood open and inviting: faded blue and smelling of mothballs. The lamps were all on, and a bright patchwork quilt lay across the bed, turned down at the corner. She looked around. There was something about the room that was off, unsettling. But she couldn't say what.

There was no dresser so she moved back and forth across the room, flinging her pants and balled-up sweaters along the closet shelves. Lily had either neglected or forgotten to clean in the back, and the corners were covered in cobwebs that stuck to her fingers. Otherwise the shelves were empty except for an old crinkled shoe box. She opened it, finding a pile of photos and old postcards instead. Adri was notoriously nosy.

She moved closer to the bedside lamp and flipped through the contents. There were several photos of a woman she assumed must be Lily, some with a man who looked to be her husband, and some of her as a little girl. But most of the mementos were older, artifacts from before even her cousin would have been born: ancient ticket stubs from shows in the 1950s, an autograph from someone named Wayne Newton. One postcard was from New York City and very old—it showed a wide boulevard with people in hats and dresses strolling arm and arm, gazing into shop windows. It was postmarked May 7, 1920, and the writing was so faded it was close to illegible.

Beth—

Arrived New York last night and making my way to you tomorrow. Galapagos in tow. Did you get my letters? Will you be waiting for me?

Will you love her as much as I do?

Love, Lenore

Adri did the quick mental math to calculate how many years had passed since 1920: a hundred and forty-five. She read it one more time, then put the box back where she'd found it.

Finally, with nothing else to do, she turned out her light and lay down. In the silence of the strange room, a feeling still nagged at her and kept her from sleeping. Maybe it was nerves about living with a stranger . . . and a stranger who was also—weirdly—family. She wondered what Lily would be like—and it made her think of her old roommate at the group house back in Miami, and something she'd said once.

"I really admire you, Adri," she'd said. "But I have to say you're not very likable."

Adri hadn't shown that it hurt her, but it had stayed in her mind. She didn't know why she couldn't keep from being too blunt, too standoffish and distant, a little mean. She'd stopped trying to change it years ago; she could never figure out how.

Growing up she'd watched other kids buddying up—everyone with their weird quirks and flaws getting along anyway somehow, forming some mysterious club she couldn't penetrate. She'd think to herself, *How do they do that?* It was like executing an intricate dive.

Adri wasn't a diver. If anything, she was a pickax, chipping away at each day. The next three months living with another stranger, even one who was related to her . . . she would chip away at too.

• • •

In sixth-grade astronomy, Adri had read about neutrinos for the first time. They were particles that traveled across space—from one end of the universe to the other, unstoppable and anchorless. They could pass through matter, right through planets and people and everything else. When kids talked after that, about what they wanted to be when they got older, the image of that textbook page always flashed through her mind.

Now she pictured the day she'd be the one launching off from Earth, unstoppable. She hoped the time between then and now would go fast. As she fell asleep, behind her eyelids she watched herself pinging across space.

CHAPTER 2

The next morning Adri woke before dawn. She tiptoed downstairs into a pastel-green hallway and took in her surroundings: walls covered in bad art—paintings of flowers and vegetables, greeting cards with angels or puppies on the front with sayings like "Hang in there!", a defunct robotic vacuum leaning against a corner, covered in dust. A magazine rack by the stairs overflowed with old newspapers, and a plush angel sat on the bottom step. Since Lily was still sleeping, Adri decided to work on the Theta.

She slipped back upstairs and quietly unfolded her small Desk Factory from its case, putting it on the nightstand beside her bed, programming it to print out the part she thought she'd need. Within moments the machine was churning out a small circuit board that she thought might do the trick. Then she crept back down the stairs and outside into the cool morning air.

But the circuit board didn't fix the Theta. Neither did a reinstall of the operating system. It had been a long time coming and, she guessed, almost perfect timing.

She patted the hood sadly. She glanced at the sky, just beginning to lighten into an orange haze. "Time of death, sunrise." The car was her most prized possession and possibly her best friend. She'd miss it more than anything or anyone else.

She turned, looking around, then veered left into the tall grass to the right of the driveway, blowing in the breeze. She wandered past the bunkhouse and into the back, where the yard gave way to fields of tall blue grass that stretched on forever and seemed to swallow a distant abandoned farmhouse.

Coming around the far side and back into the barn lot, she moved toward a small, dark bruise of a pond still engulfed in shadows. She didn't notice the low, shin-height fence until she stumbled over it, just as a movement in front of her startled her.

"Crap," she muttered. She leaned forward, her skin crawling. Something was alive at the side of the water; she could hear it scraping through the dirt. As her eyes adjusted she could make out a shape that looked like . . . what? An old shield? A huge rock? A *moving* huge rock? It was at least as tall as her knees.

She could just make out a shifting within the larger

shape—the head. It was turning to look at her. And suddenly she relaxed.

It was a turtle. A *tortoise*, she corrected herself. The big ones were always tortoises, she knew from biology. She tried to remember if they were vegetarians or not. A big bowl of water sat near the lean-to that had been built, Adri assumed, to shade her from the sun.

Adri approached the animal slowly. She stopped a couple of feet away and squatted to sit awkwardly on the low fence.

"You look cheerful," she said flatly, because the tortoise looked serious and melancholy, like most tortoises.

The creature was so large it was one step away from a miniature pony. It had a shell like a saddle, sloped and uneven and droopy looking, and a long neck, which it stuck out farther and farther now, craning to gaze at her inquisitively.

She scooted closer with an irresistible urge to lay her hands on the glinting shell and find out what it might feel like under her palm. The creature turned its head to her, snuggled against her arm.

"Oh, it's like that, huh?"

She reached toward its neck and brushed something cool and metallic. She grasped it between her forefinger and thumb: a dangling metal name tag, more like a little necklace than a collar. She squinted in the dim dawn light.

Galapagos, it read. Chills crawled up her arms.

Just then, from the corner of her eye, she saw a light flicking on in the house. She glanced one more time at the tag, took a deep breath, and headed across the yard.

The house was warm, and salsa music was playing in the kitchen. A pale, tiny, wiry lady stood at the fridge waiting for a pot of coffee to brew on its side door. She gasped as Adri entered, and her face broke into a bright smile.

"Adri!" she said, her voice rumbling, lively. "I thought you'd never get here! I'm so sorry I wasn't up to greet you."

"Um, hi, Ms. or . . . Miss Lily . . . Mrs.?" But her cousin cut her off by wrapping her thin arms around her and pulling her into a tight hug. She smelled like flowers.

"Lily," she said. "We're not fancy around here."

Adri untangled herself stiffly as Lily stood back and took her in, beaming. "How'd you sleep, honey? How was the trip?"

"I'd prefer Adri if that's okay," Adri said. She didn't like terms of endearment from people she didn't know.

Lily widened her eyes and nodded fake-solemnly, amused. "Gotcha. Did you sleep okay? Do you like your room? How are you feeling?"

"Um. Yes, yes, and good?" She accepted the mug of coffee Lily shoved into her hands.

"Well I've tried to get everything in good shape. No one's stayed in that room in years."

"I guess this place is pretty remote," Adri offered.

Lily shrugged. "Nah. It's just that I'm old and all the people I used to know are dead." She breezed on. "Cousins. *US!* Hard to believe, huh? Your great-grandpa is my mother's little brother. My mother was in her late thirties when she had me, and let's see . . . he was sixteen years younger, and when *he* had your *grandfather*, he was . . ."

Adri sipped her coffee in reserved silence as Lily bounced around the kitchen, printing eggs and bacon onto two Styrofoam plates from the KitchenLite on the counter. She kept glancing over, taking in Adri's scraggly hair, her oversized pajamas.

"Out of eggs," she said to the refrigerator. It was one of the older models that needed to be told. "So I guess you can tell I'm a talker," she said to Adri, laying the plates on the table.

"I'm not," Adri said. "Especially in the morning."

Lily nodded significantly. "I'll let you catch up with the day a little." And she made a show of zipping her lips. But she kept on staring at her as they sat down. Every once in a while she said "hmmm." And then "huh."

"What?" Adri finally asked.

Lily looked embarrassed. "Well, I was expecting you to be less . . . Well, you're a Colonist, you know, a big overachiever. I thought you'd be so . . . polished and tidy . . ."

Colonists were loved the world over, and they had been for as long as Adri could remember. As the planet's best and brightest, they spawned action figures, docudramas, and colors of eye shadow (Maybelline made silvery Phobos and purplish Deimos in honor of the two moons that circled Mars, but they also made a pink Ella and a deep-blue Lakshay for two of the best-looking Colonists who lived there). They were supposed to look the part, she supposed.

Adri didn't know what to say. "I'm in disguise," she finally said, and Lily barked a laugh.

"What's your specialty?" Lily went on. "All Colonists have a specialty, right?"

"I'm cross-trained in biology and engineering. I'll study samples and fossils. Most of us need to know how to fix stuff."

"Oh," Lily said, and wrinkled her nose. "Sounds hard."

"Having all your loved ones dead sounds hard," Adri responded, which she knew as it came out was the exactly wrong thing to say.

Lily looked surprised but not put off. She sipped her coffee. "Yeah. That's true."

Adri glanced around as they ate, uncomfortable under Lily's friendly gaze. Everything around them *sagged.* A shelf hung from one nail above the sink, ready to fall down. Two cabinets were losing their doors. The fridge—covered in angel magnets—was ancient, one of the old ones not linked to the internet so you couldn't order food. She wondered why Lily didn't have someone come fix things.

Their eyes met, and Lily put her chin on her hand. "Now . . . I know you're still waking up, but I *really* want to pin this down. I'm your dad's dad's mom's brother's daughter . . ." Lily clasped her hands together. "I saw this thing on TV about ancestry that says even personality traits can get passed through the genes. I think . . . Now are you an INTP or an ISTJ? I think you're an ISTJ . . ."

"Do I have to answer that?" Adri asked.

"No." Lily looked a little hurt, then after a few seconds, she muttered under her breath, "Probably an INTJ." Adri wondered how many genes she and Lily actually shared. They both had the same pointy chin, so it was vaguely detectable that somewhere in a giant family tree that had lost all its branches they were connected.

"Hey, Lily?"

"Yes."

"Maybe now would be a good time for me to pre-apologize. I'm not really a friendly kind of a person. I'm not charming or anything. I'm, like, the opposite of that."

"I'm gathering that," Lily said, her eyes mirthful.

"I just want you to know it's not you or anything. It's just the way I am. I really appreciate you hosting me. I'm really grateful. I just don't think we're going to be buddies or anything."

Lily studied her. She was about to speak when something drew her attention to the window. "That must be for you," she said, crossing the room and opening the front door, waving her forward. "I never get packages."

A tiny dot in the sky was getting closer and closer. Mail was coming. Just as the drone came level with the porch, it dropped its load with a thud onto the top step, and then lifted and flew back the way it had come.

Lily lifted a box and handed it to her. It read *Adri Ortiz, Colonist.* Adri's pulse sped up.

"Looks important," Lily said. "I'll give you plenty of space." She walked to the porch stairs and turned for a moment. "Who knows, you may find out I'm not that much of a friendly person either. Wouldn't it be ironic if I killed you in your sleep tonight?"

Adri stared at her in surprise.

Lily grinned and walked down into the yard.

Adri found a kind of library/TV room behind the kitchen—full of lopsided, inviting old furniture and lined with shelves bursting with old paper books. She sat on the couch and opened the box.

A Pixo lay on top, and as she held the tiny box in her palm, an image of Lamont Bell lit up above her hand, his own hands folded.

> *Welcome to Kansas! You are one of the elite individuals who has shown you have what it takes to be part of our team on Mars. We're so fortunate to have you, and I'm looking forward to meeting you! Our first session is scheduled for November 1 at 10:00 a.m.*
>
> *About a month before launch, you and I will meet individually in order to finalize your commitment. Until then, know that this is a time to confirm that we are a right fit. The next several weeks will allow you to familiarize yourself with our process, but it will also be a time for reflection. Twenty percent of our recruits find that they are unable to commit to the reality of leaving their home planet behind, and since we want only wholehearted commitment, we*

support this kind of self-inquiry.

Please arrive at the Center on time for your session.

Thank you.

Adri couldn't believe it; that was eleven days away. Why so long? She had rushed here just to hurry up and wait. She wondered how she'd survive the boredom.

The box contained a bunch of small items for her to get used to: a wearable translation filter, a Pixo containing the profiles of the other Colonists on her team . . . Adri sifted through them, and then sitting back, at a loss for what to do with herself, she turned on the TV. They were talking politics about carbon capture locations in the South China Sea. Her eyes kept going to the barn lot beyond the windows, out to where she'd been walking that morning.

Lily came back inside a few minutes later, and as she stood in the kitchen tidying up, Adri came to stand in the doorway to watch her. Inexplicably she dumped everything in the trash instead of the Cyclo-bin that stood right beside it.

"Hey, Lily?" she said. "Do you know how old that tortoise is? Galapagos?"

Lily cast a glance over her shoulder. "Old as sin. They live up to a century and a half supposedly, and I'd say she's probably pushing that."

For a moment, Adri wondered whether or not to admit she'd been snooping in Lily's box of mementos upstairs, but curiosity got the best of her.

"Last night I was looking around in my room and I found some old photos and mementos and stuff. There's a postcard. From someone named Lenore to someone named Beth. From 1920. It mentions Galapagos—it makes it sound like she was really important—like this person was coming all this way to deliver her. Do you think it's the same Galapagos?"

Lily looked up, intrigued, as she wiped down the sink. "Must be. She came with the house when my mother moved in, a lifetime ago. Along with the books, furniture . . . everything. The family that lived here, it was like they just . . . disappeared, barely took a thing with them—or at least that's how it seemed growing up." Lily fiddled with the tap, which was leaking. "My mother said they were family, but I never asked her about it, just didn't think much about it. Now that we've got no family left, I wish I had. They were Gottliebs or Godfreeds or something." She finally got the tap fixed and turned. "My mind . . ." She tapped her forehead and then smiled sadly.

Adri waited for her to elaborate.

"I've got dementia." Lily leaned back against the counter. "The other day I forgot, for a little while, that I was old. Isn't that crazy? I thought I was in my twenties and that I was looking for a job, and then I was like, oh wait a second, I retired twenty years ago." She barked out a laugh. "They say I'll start forgetting who's dead and who's alive." Her smile faded.

"I'm sorry, Lily," Adri said.

"It's the way it goes, I guess. They've got concrete that heals itself and all these diseases licked, but some things still get left behind in the dust. Just my luck." Lily looked thoughtful. "My mother had this stack of letters, about those people or from them or something—dug up when she was cleaning things out. I remember seeing her reading them on the couch a couple times, very absorbed. But I'd bet she threw them away. She was never a sentimental person."

She sighed. "It'd be nice to know why they mattered to her," she said. "How they were related to us. It'd be nice if I weren't the last Ortiz on earth, after you leave. Some family all the records missed."

They sat in silence for a while.

"You were already the last one in our family," Adri offered. "Before you knew about me, and that wasn't so bad."

"Oh," Lily shrugged. "I always knew about you. I did a DNA search years ago, and you're the only one who turned up."

Adri was taken by surprise. It made her bristle, that she'd been left in the dark. But it wasn't like she would have reached out to Lily if the knowledge had been reversed.

"Do you know Galapagos tortoises are endangered?" she said. "It's illegal for them to be pets."

Lily studied her for a second, then smiled. "We should have her arrested." She flashed a mischievous smile. "You wanna watch TV?" she asked. "There's gonna be a segment on a little girl who died and went to heaven for five minutes."

Adri couldn't imagine anything she'd less like to see. "How far is town?" she asked.

"Less than a mile. I could take you."

There was longing in her voice, but Adri ignored it. "I'm gonna go for a run."

At first there was nothing but farmland on either side of her—wheat fields and empty pastures with no houses in sight. After about two miles she passed an abandoned convenience store with windows missing and a rusting gas stand out front. But there were also signs of life: a metal sign announcing that the street had been adopted by the Rotary Club, a car-charging station, a distant ad balloon floating through the sky advertising Band-Aids. Within a mile she was passing little houses and then brick storefronts. Turning onto Main Street, she passed a grocery store that looked fairly decent, then a thrift store, a town hall, and a sanitation office. Otherwise Canaan was empty. Past town, fields of buffalo grass stretched along the side of the road and out toward the horizon.

No wonder Lily was so desperate for signs of life. She wasn't kidding when she'd said the town was dead. She was essentially all alone.

That night, after Lily had gone to bed, Adri did a cursory search around the house for the letters Lily had mentioned, but nothing turned up. She pulled out the postcard again and read it. It was mysterious, the disappearance of the family, the idea that they might be related to Lily and Adri, the turtle as a mighty gift . . . one girl asking another: *Will you be waiting for me? Will you love her as much as I do?* The words struck her as all wrong.

What was so important about a tortoise that a person would cross the ocean to deliver her? What kind of person would love a tortoise that much?

Outside her window, the moon was rising. There were astronomical observatories there now, too small and distant to see. She tried to picture her new future.

As people on whom the future depended, Colonists had access to astronomically expensive, government-controlled nanotherapies that were only available to a select few. These therapies meant a Colonist's life might go on an extremely long time. Adri looked down at her hands, trying to imagine living a century and a half, and even longer than that.

Of all the things that Adri had tried to get her head around in the past week, this was the hardest. What would living for hundreds of years be like? Did she even want to live that long? She gazed out the window and tried to picture it; she looked at her hands and tried to imagine them as three-hundred-, four-hundred-, or thousand-year-old hands.

Suddenly she realized what it was that had felt so off about the room since she'd arrived. In all her sixteen years in Miami, she'd always been able to hear the faint sound of waves and the motorboats headed across the water. She'd never slept more than a mile away from the ocean.

CHAPTER 3

For the first time that Adri could remember, she started sleeping in. She spent every morning—for the next ten days—parked on the comfy, crooked couch in the library, flipping through the channels in a haze of purposelessness—no studying to do, no devices to kill time with. She thumbed through old books (some of them so dusty they made her cough): a combination of pulp mysteries, romance novels, world history, old fairy tales, some books in Spanish, most in English. The shelves had warped a little under all the weight.

Lily seemed to accept fairly quickly that they weren't

destined to be friends and mostly kept her distance. Apparently, it took effort. She watched Adri when she thought Adri didn't notice, and she often opened her mouth to strike up a conversation before making a visible effort to stop herself. Only at meals did they talk at all about the vague outlines of their lives: Lily's husband had died ten years before. Her mother had been a single mom and had run the farm on her own. She had no siblings.

Adri was curious about her—her obsession with angels, her attachment to her lonely farm. She wanted to ask her things, but asking people things was like opening a box you couldn't close. So she was polite but not open. She answered the usual questions about her own life: Growing up in the group home had been fine. No, she didn't remember her parents. They had died in the flash floods during a cyclone, before Miami built its levy system, its floating roadways. No, she wasn't sad about it—it just was the way it was. They both went their own way most of each day.

Lily was busy enough for both of them, anyway. It seemed that, for one measly house, there was endless upkeep. She worked constantly on the yard, carrying newspapers out onto the porch in her spindly arms or pushing wheelbarrows full of mulch across the barn lot. As someone whose backyard had always been the ocean, Adri had never dreamed how much work went into owning one tiny piece of earth, pretty and peaceful as it was.

Outside, the birds flitted past the windows, hunkering down as fall set in. From the couch, there was a good view of the tortoise house, and every once in a while Lily would appear there, taking a break. Without knowing she was being watched, she'd sit next to Galapagos nose to nose, petting her and talking to her. Other times, she'd come walking into the house and startle at the sight of Adri, like she'd forgotten she was there. She'd shake the moment off, trying to hide her confusion, and Adri pretended she didn't notice.

They coexisted, and Adri began to think it wasn't going to be so bad. Still, another thing Adri had never been able to change was that people disappointed her, and Lily was no exception. It bothered her how Lily kept the heat on full blast and walked around indoors in shorts. ("You should turn the heat down, Lily. You're not on solar, and it's wasteful," she'd pointed out. Lily just said "*huh*" in response and kept it on ninety.) How she loved shows about girls going to heaven but didn't know anything about current events. And how she drove a dinosaur of a gas-devouring car.

So it made it harder when it occurred to Adri that since her Theta was dead, she needed to ask Lily for a ride to Wichita.

"I thought you said you weren't blind."

Adri clutched the armrests as Lily veered into a parking spot in front of an enormous white stone building in downtown Wichita. In the last hour she'd almost rear-ended the same car twice, chased a pedestrian out of a crosswalk ("Did you see that woman's face? I think she pooped her pants," Lily said), and driven up a small portion of a one-way street before Adri had stopped her.

Now she pulled a hat out of her purse and put it on. It was shaped like teddy bear ears.

"You look like a crazy person," Adri said.

"You look boring and average," Lily replied. She turned and climbed out of the car. She swiped her palm over the meter uncertainly as Adri climbed out of the passenger side and tried to smooth out her wrinkled button-down. She was so nervous her heart was fluttering, but she didn't know if it was from the near-death experience of the drive over or what waited inside the Center.

She took in the sights around her. Miami had been full of oceanic blues and grays; Wichita, on the other hand, was a "city of the future"—well financed and well maintained, with sleek buildings and needlelike, soaring spires rising out of the manicured greenery below.

Most of it had been built in the last fifteen years as more and more federal agencies had left Washington, DC, which was more swamp than city now. The Center, its partners from China and Nicaragua, and Plan Z—had located here because there were no floods, no quakes, no hurricanes, good infrastructure, and lots of wide open spaces to build, test, and launch.

Lily reached for her arm but pulled back as they climbed the stairs.

"You need help?" Adri asked.

"I'm trying not to invade your personal space," Lily puffed, looking small and overwhelmed as they climbed.

Adri reached for her hand. "It's fine," she said. "I'm not a *total* asshole. I don't, like, push baby strollers into the street or anything."

They were still holding hands when they checked in at a security desk, and were ushered into a long white hallway to the doorway of a crowded room, full of people Adri's age.

Lily studied the room, looking confused. "What is this place?"

Adri looked at her. "The Center. Remember?"

"Oh yeah." Lily nodded, and then smiled, amused. "Duh." She pulled her hand out of Adri's reluctantly. "I'll be outside with the other leftovers," she joked, and stepped away.

The room was buzzing with people gathered in clusters, their voices reverberating off the bright, empty walls. Adri recognized her crew mates from profiles she'd watched: Alexa, an engineer from Denver. Saba, a botanist from Kuwait. A couple of athletes who'd been training for the Olympics before they'd switched to the Institute track in kinesiology. A guy named D'Angelo who did nano-engineering, and a programmer named Shyla. With the exception of a couple of experts in their forties, they were all in their early twenties or younger. The Center chose young Colonists for their physical fitness and their likeliness to populate Mars with future generations, but Adri knew from the literature that this group was among the youngest they'd ever had.

She chose a seat near no one and adopted her standard approach of looking absorbed with something on the wall while the others introduced themselves to each other.

The lights in the room suddenly dimmed, and behind them the walls lit up with holographic pictures of Mars, so detailed and layered that it seemed you could reach your fingers in and pull out handfuls of the red dust. They were engulfed in a landscape full of enormous mountains, dizzyingly deep craters, and enormous boulders.

A moment later a man entered the room, trailed by a circle of light. A hush fell over the room as they all turned to look at Lamont Bell—midforties, dressed in a slick navy blue suit. He exuded authority, confidence, and excitement.

He laid a tablet down on the desk in front of him, swiped at the screen for a moment or two—completely unfazed by the room full of staring people—and then looked up at them all.

"I know all your faces, but it's great to meet you all in person. I want to congratulate you again on making it here; we're very happy to have you. You've been selected based not only on your abilities but also on the strength of your character, as we have been able to assess you. We want and need good people for this project. And in this room, we've got some of the best. Now, flattery out of the way, let's get to it."

He swiped at his tablet. The three-dimensional landscape

shifted, its images orbiting around them.

"Let me go over some of what you already know. Mars is a beautiful place. It contains the biggest volcanoes known to exist in the solar system, craters that make the Grand Canyon look like a pothole, breathtaking riverbeds—dry for now, but we hope not forever—and ice fields that stretch for miles."

As he spoke, he zeroed in on the features he mentioned, each image taking over the expanse of the room, making people literally take in their breath as he toggled from one thing to the next.

"It has all the elements we need to make clothes, plastic, steel, and fuel, and of course—the golden ticket—water. To date, it's relatively empty of human life, but that will change. We have four hundred and twenty-two people working on Mars, soon to be"—he looked around the room—"four-hundred and thirty-eight. These folks live in one habitat, about the size of a shopping mall." Now a dollhouse view into an elliptical dome appeared in the center of the room, with floor upon floor exposed: an apartment looking out on a dry landscape with two moons hovering above, a swimming pool, a movie theater. The next image showed a woman growing beans and cabbage under a domed Kevlar ceiling hundreds of yards above her. Then a cheesy image of a couple, each flashing the thumbs-up sign, holding a baby. People tittered.

"We've had fourteen marriages to date since the program began, and, so far, nine babies have been born extraterrestrially. We've chosen you all with compatibility in mind. I don't want to be too technical about it, I'm just saying, we think you'll jell."

Adri shifted uncomfortably in her seat because she was allergic to jelling.

"It's truly a magnificent future you are helping to create. One day we'll have transformed the atmosphere so we can walk and breathe freely anywhere on the planet. One day we'll leave the domes and take off the helmets. We are counting on you to plant these seeds.

"I'll be meeting each of you individually. At that point we'll sign contracts saying that we commit to each other: we commit that we're happy with you as a recruit and want to keep you, you commit to seeing the expedition through. This is how we protect our investment. In the next two-plus months, you'll be training with us for your new jobs. But in the meantime, we have a cheesy Vid for you. I'll see you all at Personal Sessions."

He started the Vid, the first image—of the shuttle—stretched glowingly above the room, floating three-dimensionally in the air. And then he left the room.

The Vid covered things Adri already knew: technical information about the ship, the chemical makeup of Mars, some major ways the Bubble Habitats functioned, how nature on Mars would one day be possible.

When it was over, the regular overhead lights flickered on, but an image of a one-day terra-formed Martian forest lingered in the center of the room. Adri would miss forests. Suddenly it dawned on her how many things she'd miss.

People lingered and chatted and trickled into the

hallway. Across the circle, two people laughed with each other. Self-conscious, Adri tried to follow a group out, but they hovered in the doorway talking, with her awkwardly tacked to their edge. Then someone—Saba, she thought—turned and smiled at her.

Adri tried to think of something to say. She had zero ability to engage in small talk, but she knew she was supposed to jell, so she glanced at the holographic forest and then, grasping for straws, said, "I like nature."

She wished she could swallow the words, and embarrassment flamed her face. *I like nature?*

Saba just looked confused, and Adri tried to pretend she was bored.

"See you," she muttered irritably, then slid past the group and out the door.

On the way home, Adri insisted on driving. Lily's maps didn't work, and they got lost leaving the city. They drove past the Endangered Animals Habitat, which Lily kept calling the zoo, and the same government buildings two or three times. Finally Adri managed to weave into the outskirts: green suburbs full of pleasant old houses.

Lily looked out the window, hmming and huhing to herself, clearly turning something over in her mind.

"What?" Adri asked finally, irritated. She'd tried to shake off the embarrassment back at the Center. But now she was only annoyed with herself.

"Well, I don't know how you all do it," Lily said. "I don't even know why you'd want to go to Mars in the first place."

"I want to do something that means something," Adri shot back, more tersely than she meant to. She took a breath and let it out. "People may *need* to live on Mars someday soon."

Lily nodded politely. She looked a little disinterested, or at least it seemed that way. "Huh," she said.

"It's like starting the world over," Adri pressed, trying to drive the point home, "but with more brains. Like doing it right."

Lily thought for a minute. "I'm just wondering who you're saving the world for. Since you don't seem that into people."

Adri cast a blank glance at her then turned her eyes back to the road.

"I'm just saying it's a big sacrifice," Lily mused. "It's a loving act."

Adri tried to think how to express herself. "It serves our interests to rely on each other. Love is a survival mechanism; it's evolution."

Lily rolled her eyes. "Oh geez."

It irked Adri that Lily didn't get that Colonists were envied by everyone, and deserved to be envied.

"There are huge perks," she said, her hands tense on the steering wheel. "I'll get to live for hundreds of years."

"Psh. You couldn't pay me a million dollars to live that long." Lily pushed her hands through the air as if pushing away a gift.

"Well that's good, because they only want younger people," Adri shot back.

Lily looked amused, as if she didn't know they were arguing. "Well and what's so great about younger people?" she teased.

"For one," Adri said, "we didn't use up the planet like you guys did. You know, older people."

Lily thrust her hands through the air once again, finally a little tense, her mouth tightening. "I know you young folks will get it all sorted out. I'm sure it's not so bad."

"Well there's no Miami and hardly any Bangladesh and no polar bears," Adri said tightly. "And they're paying billions of dollars to start a colony on Mars because humans need an exit strategy. So how bad do you want it to get before you think it's bad?"

Lily didn't reply for a while, and Adri looked down at her hands on the steering wheel. Instead of shaming Lily, she was acting like an idiot: she was trying to hurt an old lady's feelings, and she couldn't understand exactly for what.

"Well, you lied," Lily said finally, looking out the window.

"About what?" Adri asked.

"You *are* kind of an asshole."

A long silence followed in which Adri tried to absorb the words, which hurt but were probably true. Then Lily pinched her shoulder softly.

"That's okay, I like assholes. They're colorful."

Adri blew out a breath, exasperated.

"Can I write you? After you're gone?" Lily asked.

"Um, yeah, I guess so. We can video too. It's not, like, the 1800s. It's not like I'm taking a vow of silence."

Lily smiled. "Of course. Things are changing so fast, I lose track. I always thought that was so wonderful, the ways people are changing things. But apparently I was wrong." Her mouth turned up at the corners sarcastically.

They pulled up to the house. Lily gazed around the farm as they climbed out of the car. "My mother was an optimist. Maybe I got that from her." She cast a glance sideways at Adri. "She loved this place. And now there's hardly anyone around to remember her or the people who used to belong to her."

Adri looked out toward the tortoise house, and Lily followed her gaze. Galapagos happened, at that moment, to be staring over at them while chewing a big piece of lettuce, her eyes glittering and observant.

"Well, I guess *she* remembers," Lily said. "She's like those glasses in *The Great Gatsby*. She's seen it all, but she's not talking."

Adri hadn't read *The Great Gatsby*.

"You remind me of her a bit," Lily said. "My mom, that is. She was a force of nature too."

Adri didn't know what to say, so she didn't say anything. Compliments only embarrassed her. And she wondered why Lily was so constantly, irrepressibly nice to her.

That night, after Lily went to bed, Adri was restless, wired. When she started looking for the letters again, it wasn't with much hope of finding them, it was just an urge she couldn't explain. Maybe if she found them, she could give them to Lily as a gift—a symbolic apology for being a fairly crappy person. She went about it systematically, scouring the house—every room but the one where Lily slept—looking in cabinets, the attic (full of more junk than she'd ever seen in one place in her life), every shelf of every closet.

Finally, curled back behind a line of books, half stuffed behind a shelf that had come loose, she found a thick, bursting manila envelope, and her heart skipped a beat. It contained a clothbound journal fraying at the seams. *Property of Catherine Godspeed*, it read on the inside cover. Even staring at the name, she couldn't believe she'd been lucky enough to find it after so many years.

The first page was full of tight, scrawling handwriting. She tried to flip to the back page, but when she did, a pile of envelopes and postcards fluttered out from where they'd been tucked, landing scattered on the floor. She knelt, gathering them together in an awkward pile, and then sat back on her heels.

The letters were still neatly in their envelopes, yellowing but legible, all addressed to *Beth Abbott* (and the later ones to Mrs. Beth Godspeed), and return-addressed *Lenore Allstock, Forest Row, England.*

She carried them up to her room.

Years later, even after she'd followed the trail of it all as far as it would go, Adri would always think of that moment, kneeling in front of the bookshelves, as the moment she first touched her own history.

She sat cross-legged on her bed and opened to the first page of the journal, and read the first lines.

The dust came again this morning. It kicked up out of nowhere, looking like a gray cloud rolling across the ground instead of the sky.

She kept going. She didn't surface again until dawn.

CATHERINE

PART 1

PROPERTY OF CATHERINE GODSPEED
CANAAN, KANSAS

MAY 20, 1934

The dust came again this morning. It kicked up out of nowhere, looking like a gray cloud rolling across the ground instead of the sky. I was just walking out of the barn with a bucket when I saw it blowing across the northeast edge of the farm, but by then it was too late to get to the house. I had to hold on to the fence not to fall over my own feet, and then all those grains of dirt ran their hands against me and polished me like sandpaper, crawled into my eyes and throat. And then it passed, and the sky was that relentless blue again.

Now everything has a thin layer of grit. All Mama's books in the library are powdered. My toast this morning was dusty and so were my eggs. But we are lucky this week. Sometimes the dust blows for days.

I dream about rain and wet leaves, even when I'm awake. I could lie down on a patch of green grass and never get up.

I found this postcard in the bottom of one of Mama's drawers, while I was looking for pennies she might have left there before they became so scarce.

I've read it over six times, and I still don't understand it. There's never been a Lenore in our lives, and Mama's never mentioned her.

I can see her now, out at the side of the house, sweating over the kitchen garden—which feeds us—and Ellis, our helper over by the barn listening to baseball on his wireless, feeding our one skinny cow. Galapagos is wallowing in the mud in what used to be a pond and trying to catch a fly. Beezie is in the hall coughing on the dog.

I want to ask Mama about Lenore, but she is the best imitator of a stone you ever met. You can have a whole conversation with her just by yourself. I've spent my whole life trying to read her signals. She has a way of pulling you into her silence.

This morning she said she smells rain on the dry wind. We all looked at each other and agreed that rain is on its way. But our eyes said something different.

We're a house full of secrets. The main secret is that we are afraid.

Twenty-four sunny days in a row. Where have the clouds gone?

MAY 25, 1934

This morning in church we prayed for rain and President Roosevelt. I spend most of my time in church trying to keep Beezie from picking her nose or whispering loud and embarrassing observations like how if Jesus knew for sure he was going straight to heaven things weren't that bad for him anyway. Beezie's so tiny she may just as well be half elf, but she's a hellcat and everyone knows it. Meanwhile they barely notice me at all. Even Mama calls me her brown bird: I'm not pretty, and I blend in. But Ellis says if I'm a brown bird, I'm a vulture, for the way I circle the house in the evenings. I'm so restless I could fly out of my skin.

Ellis is the one who told me to start writing things down. At church, he sits at the end of our family bench, and when I glance his way, his head is invariably bowed. When I'm bored during the service I let myself picture him asleep in the bunkhouse—in my mind, I kiss him awake.

After service we made our way through the chattering, cheerful Sunday crowd gathered outside the church door, catching up with each other on the week's happenings. On Main Street the heat and the sun beat down on us all like a fist. As usual, everyone went out of their way to talk to Ellis. He's not a vulture but a peacock, dark-haired, always with a twinkle in his eyes like he just heard a joke, and a smile like he never met a stranger. People are drawn to him. He's the town pet.

We stopped in at Jack's store. While Mama bartered some old farm tools for flour, Ellis and I picked out other things we needed and loaded them onto the counter. I handled an apple and then put it down because the store is mostly a museum of things we can't have.

"They say the last storm blew dust all the way to New York, Beth," Jack was saying to Mama as she stood looking down at a newspaper on the edge of the counter. He looked drawn, worried, like everyone does all the time now. "They say some places in Texas, it's piled up in drifts that can cover cars."

"God will bring the rain," Mama replied. She has the slightest bit of an English accent. It always stands out. She moved here from England when she was young, and she's always said the grass there is so green and wet it looks like a carpet, that the trees that fill the woods are as covered in green as limes.

Mama is full of faith, but recently mine has been running through my fingers, dribbling out. I can't seem to catch it.

Jack's daughter Lyla darted out of the back of the store and gave us a happy wave, because like everyone else, she's in love with Ellis. The only difference is, I think he loves her back. They're both seventeen, a year older than me. Ellis likes to annoy me by calling me "the kid," but Lyla shoots him looks when he does it, standing up for me.

Ellis stepped forward, leaned on the counter, and tapped his fingers as Lyla loaded a shelf. "Any way you all can do better than three cents on this apple?" he asked, pulling it from where I'd replaced it. I was mortified, but Lyla smiled and slid it into a bag with the flour for free. That's the effect Ellis has on people. I know I'll end up giving most of it to Beezie anyway, but it still gives me a warmth inside.

Ellis was just stepping up to whisper to me when something else grabbed our attention—both at the same time.

It hung behind the cash register, tucked sheepishly below eye level: a poster, dominated by a beautiful dancing girl in a long gold skirt and big hoop earrings. Behind her were lions, a cobra twirling out of a basket, a man holding barbells, a Ferris wheel. The words *Ragbag Fair—Coming Soon!* were written across the top in red.

"Whoa," I said, gaping.

"Whoa," Ellis echoed. "Would you look at her."

I slapped his arm and shook my head. It wasn't the dancing girl I was drawn to but the picture tucked away at the upper-right corner like an afterthought: a bolt of lightning threading through a pair of gnarled old hands, and these words beside it: *Would you pay $10 for Eternal Life? You Can at the Electric! Midnight Shows Only!*

"What's the Electric?" I asked Jack.

"One of the exhibits, I guess. They'll be here for weeks, sounds like. Paid me two dollars just to hang it here, but . . ." He looked sheepishly at Mama. "I might just take it down and give the money back."

"That'd probably be best," Mama said, eyeing the poster doubtfully. Mama's a timid sort. She's never broken a rule in her life, and these kinds of carnivals are frowned on by just about everyone.

But all the way home, I was thinking about the poster—the old, wrinkled hands, the lightning bolt.

Ellis once told me that if they had a way of weighing people's souls along with their bodies I'd be 2 percent fat, 10 percent water, and 90 percent unattainable desires. (Ellis has made a lifelong career out of telling me about myself, but he can't do math.) He says I talk about rain and daydream about rain and think about rain so much that the only way I'll ever be happy is if I am reincarnated as a puddle. Every place we've ever seen a photograph of, I've told him I want to see it.

Anyway, I often tell Ellis things I'd tell no one else, but if I told him how badly I wish I had that ten dollars for the Electric, he'd laugh in my face. I want him to think well of me. He hates superstition as much as he hates cities and spinach and snakes.

Ellis came to us three years before the dust, just after Daddy died. It was the middle of a bone-cracking winter. He was eight years old, and I was seven. Farmers would meet the trains, full of orphans escaping the poverty of the cities, and pick them out like puppies.

I wasn't supposed to be there that night. Mama needed a strong, healthy, older boy to help with the heavier farm work Daddy had left behind, but I wanted a little sister so badly that I lay in the back of the truck to stow away so I could pick her out myself. (I didn't know then that Mama was carrying Beezie.)

As it turned out, neither of us got our wish. We got there too late, and there was only one child left unwanted—the right age for Mama, but pale and skinny and delicate, standing alone and coatless on the platform, shivering like crazy. When Mama offered him her coat, he said no thank you and that he wasn't cold. He was trying to look strong and dependable, but very unconvincingly. I could see the compassion in Mama's eyes.

"No," I whispered. "I don't want him. Please, Mama, no."

But I knew she'd have pity on him, like the little birds the cats are always after, and the little newborn calves I've seen her puff back to life with her own breath.

"Well," Mama said, after we stood there in front of him for a few minutes. "Come with us."

The first thing I said to him, once we were in the truck—him sitting in the back and still not wrapping his arms around himself—was "We wanted a girl."

He had the good nature to look sorry. I've been in love with him ever since.

Now he loves Canaan more than maybe even Mama does. He says the day he got off the train in this town was the luckiest day of his life.

MAY 28, 1934

I only have a moment to write this. I've asked Mama about the postcard.

It was late yesterday afternoon. We'd just finished gumming clean sheets over the windows after four days of dusters. The best time to talk to her about anything is when her hands are busy, when she sometimes lets her thoughts run free.

"Mama," I asked. "Who is Lenore?"

Her hands paused on the windowsill, and then she resumed her work. "She was an old friend." And then, as if she'd thought better of leaving it open-ended, she added, "She died."

"A close friend?" I asked.

She sat back on her heels and studied me. "No," she said. "No, not really. I knew her in England, when I was very little. We drifted apart after that."

"Oh," I said.

She squeezed me on the shoulder then went back to work. Squeezing me and Beezie is her way of telling us how much she loves us because she's not the kind of person who says it.

And that was it. She made a show of being done, left the room, washed up her brush and bucket, and went upstairs to her room. Like I said, talking to her can be like talking to a stone. At least she didn't ask where I got the name in the first place.

But last night, when I went down for some milk after bed, I heard something shuffling in the pantry. At first I thought it was a mouse, but then I heard someone sniffing. The walls are thin, and to avoid waking us upstairs, she'd closed herself in there to cry.

The wind is back again. I've come to hate the sound of it.

JUNE 5, 1934

I'm sitting here at the edge of the mudhole pond, perched on a rock, putting off cleaning the chicken coop. There's only a slight breeze drying the sweat on my skin; the sun is blazing. The windmill across the yard is spinning, but where it used to churn up water it just creaks and spins the dust. Still, our home is beautiful even now. You can see all the way to the edge of the earth, it feels like.

I've been reading *Jane Eyre* but finished it too fast. I'm so desperate for excitement I've committed to reading every one of Mama's books in the library, but at this rate I'll be through them in a few months. We'll never be able to afford another book after that, and then I'll just have to stare at the walls.

In front of me, Galapagos and Sheepie are bickering like an old married couple. We don't let Sheepie run free anymore because last week the Chiltons next door lost their dog, Blinkers, in a storm, so to pass the time he's started trying to herd Galapagos. Right now she's gazing at him with what could only be called amused disgust. Nobody can get Galapagos to do anything she doesn't want to do.

I wonder about her now, after the postcard. Over the years, Mama's made her several little wooden overhangs for shade on the best side of the pond. And though we've had to cut back on so many things—only have three chickens left and one sad cow—she brings the turtle buckets of water to drink and cool her feet. She shares with her our meager tomato crop, blackberries she's managed to find or buy, or anemic lettuce leaves she's clawed out of the spindly garden.

"She's just a teenager," she says. "She needs her food."

And it's as if Galapagos knows she's royalty. She likes to sun herself and forage around in the morning, bask for a bit in the sun, and then head for shade and watch us work, craning her neck like she's watching an interesting play.

Still, I'm not writing because of Galapagos, but because of what Mrs. Chilton said this morning when she came over. She was standing there in our kitchen, scuttling her two youngest children away from Beezie—who was extravagantly coughing on all her dolls to make sure they wouldn't play with them. (Beezie's had the cough for weeks, and often uses it to evil purpose.)

The kitchen was full of the static that comes with the dust, and we were all trying to avoid rubbing against each other as we moved around the small kitchen so we wouldn't get sparks. (In the worst storms, the charge in the air has been known to short cars.) Mrs. Chilton has seven children, so her hair always looks like she's just been shocked anyway. She once said to Mama, "Cathy isn't much to look at, but you won't find someone who works harder," but I don't hold it against her because I know she's too tired to think straight.

"David's talking about going west," she said, and sipped at her tea, trying to pass it off as a casual statement. "He says he can't take the poison air. He's worried about little Lizzie."

"What's that?" Mama asked evenly, as if she didn't know what the west was. She was pounding the life out of a ball of dough. It had been quite a day already because Beezie had torn down the sheets we spent all day plastering and then blamed it on Sheepie. When we pointed out they were covered in her dirty handprints she knelt by Sheepie and lifted one of his paws and tried to convince me that paws look exactly like hands. The dog is her best friend, but it's not the first time she's tried to pin her crimes on him.

"That's what I said *to him.* Going west would be like jumping into a black hole. What do we have to live for out west? People hate us there."

Which I know is true. They call us Okies no matter what state we're from. They make laws to keep us out.

Mama wiped her hair out of her face with her wrists. "The weather will change soon."

"That's what I told him, Beth," Mrs. Chilton agreed. "Mark my words, we'll never leave that house as long as I live. I may as well die as leave. This is home."

Mama went on silently with the dough. She's always taking in information and rarely giving it, and this leads people to think she either agrees or disagrees with them, depending on their mood. But I know Mama is as likely to leave Canaan as she is to leave her own bones behind. Every time I've tried to bring up that we should cut our losses and go (before the dust drowns us), she's conjured up a thousand reasons why we can't: that we have no money and barely anything left to sell, that things are no better in the cities—no jobs, businessmen selling fruit on the street to live, influenza running rampant, and we don't know a soul anywhere but here. All of this is true, but still I disagree.

"This town used to be a paradise," she has said many times, "and it will be a paradise again, if we can just hold on." She shakes off the gloom, or tries to, with a toss of her head. "We've had so many bad years; the good ones are coming. God wouldn't be mean enough to have it otherwise.

"You've always been restless," she adds.

It's been four years since it all started, since the rain dried up, first just a few dry weeks here and there and puffs of dust swirling around. It feels like yesterday that every farm was wheat all the way to the horizon.

I remember I used to feel that we were the luckiest people on earth. Like that was just who we were, and it would never change. We'd see other people—dragging through town looking for work, people who couldn't get hired on account of their background or prejudice toward their skin color or their threadbare clothes—and feel like we were two different kinds of human beings, the lucky and the unlucky, the people who were naturally happy and prosperous and the people who weren't. We were fools.

There was a time Mama would say she dreamt of going back to England, to see where she grew up, and I used to believe her. But now I suspect—despite the terrible uncertainties beyond Canaan—that the main thing is she believes happiness is something behind her, to remember instead of to chase.

I'd still consider leaving if it were just me alone. God knows I'd be a fool to stay for Ellis, who'll marry Lyla someday and set up on his own.

But we are like one person, the three of us: me as the brains and busy hands, and Beezie as the beating heart, and Mama as the soul we could never unwind from ourselves. We'll probably die right here one day sweeping the front room together. We'll just be skeletons with brooms in our hands. We—

LATER—

In bed now, thinking how I'd give anything for a piece of ice to hold against my cheeks. Sheepie is shivering and obsessing and trying to herd me out of the room. There must be a storm nearby because I just rubbed my stockings against the bedspread and there was a crackle and a pop.

I had to stop writing because Ellis came walking up to help me with the coop.

"I like doing it," he said. "I have a technique."

"Your nostrils flare when you lie," I said, picking up my shovel and digging into the smelly waste at the bottom of the coop. The truth is I'm terrible at tasks like this: tasks that involve patience—I'm impatient in body and soul. I'm always knocking my elbows against the walls as I turn corners because it takes too long to steer my way around.

"You must watch me a lot to know something like that, kid," he said, smirking. "Are you planning to declare your intentions toward me? Are they honorable?"

"Don't be stupid," I said and dug in my shovel.

For a long time we worked in silence, clearing the sawdust and muck, laying new sawdust.

After a while Ellis spoke, as if picking up the thread of a conversation we were already having. "She must have other letters somewhere, if that girl was so important to her. She's hiding something."

I'd told him about the postcard from Mama's room and how I heard her crying. I tell him almost everything, and I've never told him a problem I had that he didn't try to fix.

"Maybe." Preoccupied with other things, I hadn't thought about it much since we'd talked. I stood straight to rest for a moment and rubbed my arm along my forehead.

"That's a good look for you," Ellis teased, indicating with his finger that I'd swiped some muck across my forehead by mistake. He traced the line of it without touching his finger to my skin.

I winced and turned my face away, embarrassed.

He studied me, his brows drawn down over his eyes. "Sorry," he said. "I'm not contagious, I swear." His teasing, unfolding smile tugged a smile onto my own lips. Ellis has that effect on people. He recently pickled some tumbleweed and got us to eat it. He said we need the minerals. Anyone who can get you to eat pickled tumbleweed can get you to do anything.

We finished up, and I looked at him for a moment, too tempted to keep silent anymore. "I don't need to find some old letters. I need to find a way to make ten dollars," I said.

He studied me for a moment in confusion.

"Why?"

"I just do."

"That's an impossible amount of money, Cathy. For any of us."

"I know," I said hopefully.

He stuck his hands in his pockets. "I'll think about it," he said. Simple as that.

There are so many things I don't like about Ellis. I don't like the way he licks his lips when he concentrates. I don't like how he won't daydream with me about being millionaires or going away ("There's no better place than here," he says). Everyone would think out of the two of us, he's the stronger one, but they'd be wrong. These are the things I tell myself when I feel most desperate to have him, when he is the most kind and tender and irresistible.

But nothing works. I always know where he is without looking—my eyes track him even when I want them not to. I imagine that I stumble upon him by the cow pond, or in the clearing at the edge of the property, and in my dream he looks at me like it hurts too much not to touch me. And we kiss. We more than kiss. If there were a God who cared how much any of us want or need anything, he would make it rain and he'd make Ellis Parrish love me.

Beezie is coughing in her sleep down the hall, and whatever storm was nearby must have passed because Sheepie is now happily chasing a fly around the room. In the moonlight the dying tree in the front yard looks like it's wearing a halo.

JUNE 16, 1934

So many grasshoppers floating on the air today. I'm watching them through my bedroom window, and they fill me with dread. But I want to write this down while it's vivid in my mind.

Last night I went to the Electric.

Yesterday began with three families missing from Sunday service. It's no secret that they won't be coming back. Too ashamed or sad or impatient to say good-bye, they've simply disappeared, leaving abandoned farms behind them. It happens more and more.

Last night I lay awake thinking of them with a sharp, desperate feeling in my chest; I don't know if it was worry or envy. I kept thinking, what if they don't make it where they're going? What if they do?

Too hot and tortured to sleep, I slid out of bed.

I didn't intend to go to the Ragbag Fair at first. When I pulled on clothes and my shoes and tiptoed out the front door onto the porch a little before eleven, I was setting out toward Ellis.

I walked across the grass and stood outside his door. I was daring him. I stood there with my heart in my throat, the thought of him so close pounding in my head. I shuffled my feet in the dirt. I was thinking if he heard me and came outside, I'd do something brave.

As the minutes passed, my nerves settled. He wasn't going to come. I gazed down the drive. The full moon was up high above the trees, and the drive was lit so brightly it could have been a sandy beach.

I turned my feet toward town and started walking.

The first thing I saw, approaching the edge of the fair, was the tall, illuminated clock at the center of the grounds, surrounded by booths offering everything from piglet racing to candy apples to Shoot the Can. Organ music drifted out on the air. I made my way past a billboard painting of a man aiming a cannon upward. *Experience the Wonder of the Rainmaker!* it exclaimed. *TNT will squeeze RAIN out of the Sky!*

Though it was close to midnight, the crowds were still lively. I gaped at one thing after the next, brushing past people devouring the food, chatting and laughing, trying their luck at games of chance. Many were trickling toward the back of the grounds and gathering near a tattered red tent.

I faded into the noisy group as it pressed itself around the tent. A small, simple sign out front announced that this was what I'd come for. This was the Electric. All around me, people turned their faces to the clock at the center of the grounds.

As the minute hand approached twelve, everyone went quiet. And then, exactly at the stroke of midnight, the flaps of the tent parted and a man—middle-aged, trustworthy looking—emerged, stepping up to a small wooden podium. He was not flashy, not handsome. He had no top hat or blinding white smile. He was bald, in a threadbare suit, stooped and tired looking, like so many of the men in the crowd. He cleared his throat and looked around at all of us with kind gravity.

"It is a time of upheaval and uncertainty," he began. "The world is changing beneath our feet. Death is around every corner. Fear and despair lurk in every house." People around me murmured agreement. I crossed my arms to stave off a chill. "But it is possible to outrun it," he went on, thrusting one finger slowly up in the air, "to outstrip it, to outsmart it."

He lifted something from behind the podium, covered in a velvet blanket. He sighed as if exhausted. "I have before you something rare in these lean, rational, and industrial times. *A magical object.* One that combines the best of both worlds . . . the old and the new. Developed by researchers in New York City, it is the perfect union of the Earth's ancient power and man's genius."

"Now let's see." He lifted the blanket as if scared of burning himself, and he revealed a glass ball pulsing with light. The crowd around me gasped; I felt as if my own breath had been sucked out of me. It looked as if he'd captured lightning and put it in a fish bowl.

"*Electricity.* It's the substance at the heart of the universe. It's the origin of the heartbeat. We, you see, are *electrical* creatures. Even the world's most cool-headed scientists would tell you as much." He squinted thoughtfully and licked his lips in concentration. His eyebrows drooped as if he were carrying the weight of the world.

"Now you may ask, why have I gathered you at this late hour to see it? At midnight? Because midnight is the permeable hour. Yes." He nodded, as if to himself. "Time matters. *Time matters.* In nature's calendar, midnight is the breath between day and night. It's only at this hour that neither the sun's rays nor the moon's great pull can interfere with the electrical currents."

He looked up at all of us, wiped sweat off his forehead with his sleeve, and then laid the ball of light down on a special stand beside the podium.

"Touch this—Earth's most powerful substance—but tempered by glass so it won't kill you—for five seconds and it'll cure your ailments. If you have a sore back, a trick knee that aches when it rains . . . you'll feel better instantly. If you touch it for ten seconds, it will rejuvenate your organs. Lay your hands on it for a full minute, and it is entirely possible you could live for much longer than is thought to be humanly possible. Ladies and gentlemen, I believe this device just might help you live forever."

He paused, gazed around at us, looking exhausted. "I've made it my life's work to deliver this once-in-a-lifetime opportunity to everyone I can. I'm traveling the world in hopes of lighting up every dark corner with hope by dispelling the tyranny of death. And I'm here today to do that for *you.*

"For the next four weeks this fair is in your town, I'm offering you a chance at immortality. And all I ask is a small donation to cover travel costs and food for me and my assistants, so we can afford to reach people everywhere. The question is, are you willing to donate ten dollars in exchange for the most priceless thing imaginable?"

There on the spot, people began to line up. It seemed the professor would go on, but, looking down at them, he cut himself short and stepped down the stairs. He slid through a flap into the tent.

A murmur went through the crowd. Some who weren't in line already walked away, others stayed and milled around. The man next to me muttered that it was all nonsense and stalked off.

But I wanted to be inside the tent so badly I could taste it.

Have to go. Someone's coming up the drive.

LATER, SAME DAY

I've moved out to the mud pond. Beezie's just come to sit beside me, and she's playing in the dirt, coughing into a handkerchief so every once in a while I put my pen down and slap her on the back as hard as I can to help her get it out. I didn't know it was possible to hate anything as much as I hate the mud coming out of her lungs. (She's a mud pie all over. Dirt in her hair and on her bare arms and legs that we can never wipe off because there's always more settling on us.)

The doctor from the Red Cross says that yes, it's the dust, and to regum the windows.

Our visitor was a complete surprise. It was Lyla, who's never come out to the farm.

"I've been wanting to check on you all," she said, grinning brightly as I walked down the drive to meet her. "See how you're getting along out here."

"Thanks." I was flattered, then I began to notice she was looking over my shoulder more than into my eyes, and then it sank in and I felt like a fool.

"Would you like to see Ellis?" I asked.

Her face lit up even more if that's possible. I wondered to myself how Lyla does not seem to sweat.

"I'll get him," I offered, still liking her despite seeing through her. But as we turned I saw Ellis was already on his way out of the bunkhouse, rubbing the hay and dust out of his hair.

He didn't meet my eyes as we three stood there talking, mostly about meaningless things, and some things that are hard to write. I left them as soon as I could without being rude.

And now here I am with Galapagos again, and Beezie is beside me marching her only doll—ugly and eyeless—through the dust.

"She's trying to steal him away from you," she whispered to me a few minutes ago.

"Beeziegirl," I whispered back, "he's not mine to steal."

I've been sitting here looking out over the landscape, trying to convince myself that I love our land more than I love Ellis anyway.

Anyway, the news from town occupies my mind.

Lyla said that this week she saw two people shake hands and knock each other over from the static electricity that passed between them.

The other thing she told us is something I can barely stomach to think about: a man who goes to our church was found under the dirt two days ago, dead. He'd gotten caught up in a duster while driving to Wichita and tried to run to safety from his car. He got buried alive.

JUNE 24, 1934

Storms every day this week. We sit in the living room wearing the masks the Red Cross gave us and pray for the winds to stop. Only Sheepie refuses to take shelter—she stays out by the pond trying to herd Galapagos into her little house. Mama keeps saying we ought to move the tortoise inside, but—tucked inside her dust-crusted shell—she weathers the storms better than anyone.

This morning, when all was finally calm, Mama sent me to check on the Chiltons. The dust was up to my knees in places and getting across the pasture that separates our properties was like trudging through snow.

I knew right away that something was off. Maybe it was the quiet, or that the windows were dim on a dark day, or maybe I *felt* the absence of them.

My feet echoed as I climbed up onto the porch. I knocked, then opened the door and called inside, but no one answered. Going farther in, I found utensils scattered on the floor, jars overturned, hardly any belongings gone. It was like they'd just walked out the front door, knocking a few things over in their hurry, and kept going.

I can't remember a time I didn't know them.

A husk of jackrabbits darted out of a low trough in front of me as I made my way home and made me leap with surprise. My heart was pounding. Reluctant to tell Mama and see the sadness on her face, I turned for Ellis's bunkhouse instead.

By the time I reached his door I was so preoccupied that I walked right in without knocking and then came up short.

He was standing beside Lyla, very close to her. They were talking in low tones and looking at something on his dresser, and both turned to look at me like I'd burst in on a secret.

"Sorry," I said, mortified, and turned to hurry out. I could feel Ellis's eyes on my back all the way up to the house.

Mama took the news stoically. She didn't say a word.

"Mama, don't you worry about Beezie?" I asked softly, feeling the hard knot of fear in my throat. My hair stood like duck fuzz on my arms. It's a thing she and I don't talk about, but we hear it everywhere: children fare the worst. "Shouldn't we go too?" We can go east or west, south or north, I don't care which, as long as we go.

Mama sat with the tips of the fingers against her lips, staring distantly out the window. She wouldn't meet my eyes. She impersonated a stone.

I've been sitting here thinking about how the Chiltons have

had the courage to save themselves. As for the rest of us, I believe more than ever we will be chewed up until there's nothing left of us. Starting with the smallest first.

JUNE 27, 1934

I can't stop sinning. It's the same every night.

I get in my bed meaning to stay, but I lie here in the heat, wide-eyed. Sometimes I actually think I can hear the Ragbag music drifting out from town, and my feet slide out of the covers and onto the floor like I'm a puppet being dangled along by the moon. I get dressed and walk the starlit distance with a single thought in my head—getting to see the Electric again.

I watch the people—those with more money than we have or more reckless with what they have, or the ones too desperate to care—step up and take their chance, disappearing into the tent.

I don't know why I need so badly to watch them. I think that after each day making me a little smaller inside, those night hours walking into town and knowing I will see people emerge from the professor's tent saying they're healed—makes me feel like I've escaped something. I feel like I've gone beyond these tiny outlines of myself.

I know I'll never see England or China and never have Ellis and never be rich. So I want to hold that ball of lightning in my hands. I want my chance at living too, and this is as close as I can get.

This morning, just before dawn, I woke to Ellis throwing pebbles up at my window.

"What?" I whispered out to him once I got the window up. Of course, I thought he may have come to confess his secret love for me.

He held his hands out to the sides as if I should take him in in all his glory.

"I've got the money," he said simply, and then walked off toward his morning chores.

JUNE 28, 1934

Yesterday I was hollow-eyed and hungry washing clothes (we do it rarely and pour the used water onto the garden), when a man came to get our last cow, who's been too starved to make milk. I don't like to think what he plans to do with her.

In the afternoon Ellis caught up with me on the porch and pulled a wad of wide green bills out of his pocket with a flourish, crisp and folded once.

"Where'd you get it?" I asked, staring.

"It doesn't matter," he said.

I shoved the money back at him. "If you stole it I . . ."

He shook his head. "Of course I didn't steal it. Have a little faith."

I waited. He could see I was digging in my heels, waiting for an explanation.

"Where do you go at night?" he asked. "Tell me your secret, and I'll tell you mine."

I shoved the money into my apron pocket, turned back to sweeping, and said breezily, "What are you talking about?"

"I saw you, Cathy. Trailing in close to dawn."

I felt my skin heating up. I leaned back on my heels.

"Are you meeting someone? A boy?" he asked. I tried to detect a glimmer of jealousy on his face, but his look was only stern.

"Of course not." For a moment, we stood at an impasse.

I knew he wouldn't approve of the foolishness of it. But I also knew he'd never take the money back, so what did I have to lose? What should it matter what Ellis thinks of me?

"I'll take you when I go," I finally said, surprising myself. After all, I owed him. "Tonight. Eleven o'clock."

Ellis blew a breath through his teeth and put his hands behind his head, grinning. And now I'm in bed watching the moon rise outside the window, waiting for time to pass.

JUNE 29, EARLY MORNING

I should have noticed right away: walking to Ellis's bunkhouse last night, it was so dark I nearly walked right past it . . . and it's never that dark anymore.

I was too excited. I felt my way to the door, tiptoed into his room, and knelt by his bed to shake him awake.

"Cathy," he whispered, his eyes fluttering.

"Do you want to go or not?" I asked, breathless to be so close and alone, leaning back on my heels. His room, the whole world with me included, was an oven.

He shook off sleep, sat up, and turned on the lamp.

"Turn around," he said, and I faced the wall while he got dressed.

The lamp shed a dim glow onto Ellis's few belongings. I never go into his room, but now I saw the few things he has on his simple dresser: a framed photo of me, Beezie, and Mama, a book I gave him that he never read, a bracelet I wove for him out of straw once. These were the things he and Lyla Pearl had been looking at. I was taking it all in when I heard the sound. At first, sickened, I thought it was footsteps—Mama catching us. But it was too fast and light. The sound was strange and exotic but also achingly familiar. Ellis and I looked at each other in confusion.

I stepped to the door and squinted into the darkness outside and let out a cry.

I've been sitting here thinking how to write about it. Words keep flitting in and out of my mind, none of them right or enough.

We were outside before we could catch our breaths again, standing with our hands up. Then it made sense, the darkness of the night, the absence of the moon: clouds had blotted out the light. We stood there with our faces up to them, mystified and amazed; if they'd been dragons we wouldn't have been any less in awe of them. We opened our mouths to catch the rain.

It came down harder and harder, and all I could think was, *Don't stop.* The ground at our feet swallowed the moisture like a sponge.

Static crackled along the fence. Thunder rumbled loudly, and lightning flared somewhere in the distance. Ellis and I ducked back inside, slid to the wall beside the door. His hand on my elbow was shaking, and I wondered why.

"Stop shaking," I said nonsensically. Ellis laughed as if it were the most ludicrous request in the world, which it was.

"I'm nervous," he said.

It was only lightning, I thought. But his hands had moved to the bottom of my rib cage. His fingers sparked against the fabric of my clothes.

I'll try to record it as clearly as I can, because God knows I've relived the moment a hundred times in my mind already: Ellis was lightly brushing the edges of his hands along the tops of my arms. Even then I thought I was misunderstanding, as silly as that seems. The room seemed to get smaller, and I couldn't breathe. I didn't know for sure until his lips were against me—first the side of my cheek and then quickly after, my lips.

"Sorry, kid," he said, which made no sense because he kissed me again.

He leaned back. We stood there for a moment close together, and I looked everywhere but at him, until a noise came from the direction of the house, a kind of *whoop!* Ellis cocked his head and whispered, "We better go." He reached for my hand and tugged me gently outside into the rain. A light had gone on upstairs, and a moment later Beezie and Mama appeared on the porch. Beezie launched into furious circles around the yard, screaming with glee as she got drenched. Mama hurried to my side, hugged me around my neck, her face lit up like a little girl's—happier than I'd ever seen her.

"Rain!" she whispered.

It wasn't long before the drops began to flag. We held out our hands to prove it wasn't true, but the rain was slowing down. And then, only a few minutes after it had begun, it stopped altogether.

Still, we couldn't stop smiling, though I was shaking from what had happened.

"See?" Mama said. "We just have to believe. Everything's gonna be all right."

We waited a while longer for it to come back until, reluctantly, Mama and Beezie and I headed toward the house and Ellis toward the bunkhouse. I couldn't bring myself to look back.

I've just woken up, and every single cloud was gone from the sky. Three thoughts circled around my mind all night and wouldn't let me sleep:

Did he mean it?

Does he regret it?

Will it happen again?

JUNE 30, 1934

I was heading down the stairs this morning, just after I last wrote, when I heard a scream in the front yard. It was a kind of wailing. I thought it was an animal at first.

I rushed outside in confusion to find Beezie in the front yard, staring at the ground, with Mama kneeling beside her.

Sheepie lay on the dirt at her knees, dead.

Mama was doing something strange that I couldn't make sense of. She had a knife at Sheepie's chest.

"Don't do that! Don't do that!" Beezie pleaded, but Mama, her face dark and sad and determined, ignored her.

I stepped up and covered Beezie's eyes, suddenly understanding. I knew why, horrifying as it was to see our beloved Sheepie like that, it needed to be done.

We needed to know for sure what she'd died of.

But of course we all knew before Mama was even finished, before all the dark muck poured out of the slit in her skin Mama had made.

Her lungs were full of mud.

All this time, she's been slowly suffocating.

A moment later, Ellis emerged from the bunkhouse in a daze, and as we exchanged a look, Beezie ripped out of my arms and ran to the edge of the mud pond, where Galapagos stood craning her neck to watch us. Beezie started throwing rocks at her. "I wish it was you," she yelled, as Galapagos hissed and ducked into her shell. I picked her up and carried her inside, kicking and screaming and coughing the whole way.

JULY 2, 1934

It's been two days since Sheepie died, and the house has been dark and sad. Beezie won't come out of her room and has dressed herself all in black, her pale, grieving face peeking out from under Mama's black church hat. Not that we all aren't mourning Sheepie, but seeing Beezie mourn him hurts worse.

I have been thinking about the Ragbag fair. I've been trying to accept what entered my mind the moment I saw Sheepie dead, and what it means I need to do.

Ellis and I weren't alone until this morning. I'd found a quiet spot in the barn to sit and hide, and he came walking up beside me.

I didn't look at him. He sat down next to me, folded his hands between his knees.

Despite what had happened, the moment was comfortable between us, I guess because Ellis has always been a good listener to my silences. I never feel like I have to say something to him to be heard, and it's been like that since we were kids. But after a while, I needed to ask him.

"Do you think Beezie's lungs look like that inside?"

"No." He shook his head.

I studied his face. I didn't have to say that I knew he was lying. After a while, he looked up at me gravely.

"I made a mistake, kissing you," he said. "I think I was just so happy about the rain."

I nodded vigorously and falsely. "I know," I said. "Me too."

"You're like a sister to me."

"I know. Me too," I lied. I didn't want him to feel guilty. I didn't want to look like a fool.

He seemed to be trying to read my face. He rose onto his

knees to get up, and I looked at my hands and tried to swallow the sting of it.

"I told myself I'd be brave about it and tell you the truth."

"Yes." I nodded, withering up.

He hesitated, started to move away, but stopped himself. Then again he was doing things I couldn't make sense of. He put one hand on either side of me in a way that was not brotherly, leaned over top of me and looked at me uncertainly, hopefully, and then kissed me again. Then he said something that made my heart pound more.

"I've loved you so much, Cathy," he whispered, as his hands raced up the sides of my rib cage. "For so long. That's the truth."

I'd gone watchful and still without meaning to, a statue like Mama. Ellis sank back and looked at me miserably. "You don't feel the same way about me," he said softly.

I slowly put my hands on his chest then on his shoulders, getting a feel for it, for being allowed.

Ellis laughed a nervous laugh.

We kissed again and again and again until my lips hurt, and all I wanted was for them to hurt more.

It's been an hour since then and I can see in the mirror that my lips are still too red from all the kissing.

JULY 5, 1934

Even the letters of the words I'm trying to write feel thrilling—the curves of the e's and the t's that spell out the speck of a beauty mark under his eye, the imperfect curve of his collarbone (once broken on one side, before we knew him), the way his smile between kisses is a half smile and half unhappy wish for more.

We piece together the story between kisses.

He says how I never showed the slightest sign of feeling that way for him. "Everything you want is always written all over you," he said, his head was on my shoulder. "I looked for it so many times, but it wasn't there. I didn't know you could keep secrets like that, Cathy."

I've never been accused of being stoic.

"I honestly didn't think the thought of me like that had ever crossed your mind," he went on.

"It has crossed my mind," I said, kissing one corner of his lips, then the other.

Since then, several times yesterday and today, we've found ourselves moving toward the same shadowy places to hide from the heat and from Mama.

Mama sleeps in a chair every night, down in the parlor. Since Sheepie, worry keeps her staring out the windows, until she nods off, exhausted. But some night soon, she'll make it back to her bed. And that's when I'll take my chance to make the long walk into town with my money in my pocket.

JULY 6, 1934

Yesterday we did our chores and circled around each other, and when he went into the bunkhouse at lunch, biting my nails, I followed him. He was waiting around the doorway for me.

He took a wet cloth and rubbed the dust off my lips. He put Vaseline under my nose where it was raw.

I told him I love him over and over, whispering it in his ear, and each time he held me tighter, and each time the words felt better on my lips.

I reached into my pocket and gave him a perfect, round white pebble I'd found earlier in the day. (Gifts are hard to come by in Canaan.) He reached under his bed, where he brushed some dirt aside and lifted two of the roughhewn planks from the floor.

"I made a hiding place," he explained. He pulled out a small wooden box and opened it, laying the pebble inside. I could see the box contained two quarters and a broken pocket watch, the only thing he'd arrived in Canaan with.

"This is where I keep my treasures," he joked. "Including my vast savings. Or what's left of them. And now all my favorite pebbles."

"Who are you hiding it from?" I asked, amused.

Ellis stared into the box. "Old habit, I guess, from before I came here. I just like to know it's all tucked away where only I can find it," he said. "It makes me feel safe."

I felt guilty, seeing the mostly empty box. He didn't have much to save.

I keep my plans from Ellis. Every time we're together, I unravel myself for him, show him almost everything about me. But the Electric, I keep to myself. I can't stand the thought, now, of how he would look at me if he knew.

JULY 7, 1934

Last night, Mama slept in her room. I watched her go to bed, and my heart began to pound.

Around eleven I tiptoed into Beezie's room and got her out of bed, dressed her, and bundled her down the stairs in my arms. Thankfully she was too groggy to ask questions. I snuck past the bunkhouse with her on my back.

The Ragbag Fair was, if possible, more crowded than last time. A wooden trailer I'd never noticed stood to our left as we entered, painted with promises of what lay inside: a mermaid, a wolf man, a woman with the world's longest fingernails. Crowds were making their way up the stairs. The piglet races were on; we could hear the announcer above the crowd, and the carousel spun brightly as we walked past it.

"Why are we here, Cathy?" Beezie whispered into my ear, her arms tight around my neck.

"We're here because we need to be," I said nervously.

All through Professor Spero's talk, the mood was different than that first night. The buzz of excitement was gone. The mood was heavier, people more urgent and more desperate. When the time came, I took Beezie's hand and we went to stand in line.

Inside, the tent fell short of my expectations. An assistant stood just inside, taking the "donations." The main attraction was just a table at the center of the room and the electric ball at the center of the table. Professor Spero sat behind it, speaking to people as they sat down, then taking their hands gently in his and laying their fingers on the ball for the amount of time they'd paid for. When it was our turn, I guided Beezie into the chair. The professor smiled wearily. I had a hollow, nervous feeling as he reached for Beezie's hands.

Despite the fact that I don't pray anymore, I prayed.

And I watched Beezie take my chance at living forever.

"Do you feel better?" I asked a few minutes later, when we'd emerged into the open air.

To my relief, Beezie nodded, her chubby cheeks pink with excitement (her cheeks are never pink anymore, so I take it as a good sign). "I think so," she said breathlessly. "I feel a lot better. Almost completely better."

I only happened to look up when she did, following her eyes to see Ellis standing under the big clock, watching us.

We were halfway home. Ellis hadn't said a word, and I was too prideful to ask him, until the words burst out of me.

"What's wrong?"

He gave me a look like the answer was obvious, which it was, and tightened one hand around Beezie's ankle, the other around her wrists that crisscrossed in front of his neck.

"I can't read your eyebrows," I said.

He stopped walking for a minute, opened his mouth a few times to say something, then started walking again. "You can't expect me to be happy about spending my money on something so . . ." His eyes darted to mine, then away. Like saying it took a lot of effort.

"So what?"

He didn't answer.

"I'll pay you back."

This brought him to a full stop.

"First, you can't, and second, I don't want the money, Cathy. I'd give you more than that if I could, everything I have. It's the waste. I saved that money for a year! How could you throw it away on something so . . . flimsy? Something for idiots?"

I felt the ice in my feet again. I felt right and wrong all at the same time.

"Beezie says it worked," I said. "It's going to help her lungs."

"That's the most nonsensical thing I ever heard."

"It's scientific." I felt my cheeks heating with humiliation.

"It's *pretend*."

"You don't know anything about anything, Ellis. You've never even read a whole book."

He stopped for a moment, and his face hardened. "Well I do have common sense."

I swallowed whatever arguments I had ready. I couldn't defend myself. What other argument could I make for the promise of the Electric to be real except that I needed it to be?

"And to put Beezie through it," he went on. "That's the worst part. To give her false hope."

"It wasn't for her initially," I shot back.

He bit his bottom lip thoughtfully, his eyes sad, and shook his head.

We walked the rest of the way in silence, Beezie still sound asleep, and then slowed in front of Ellis's door, lingering in the dark and looking at each other.

Ellis let go of Beezie's foot and suddenly slid his hand into mine. Like we'd done it a hundred times. "Cathy . . . ," he whispered. But I quickly pulled my fingers away. I reached for Beezie, to gently pull her off his back, and held her snug in my arms. She lay her head limply on my shoulder.

"What if it actually helps?" I asked. "What if it turns out to be true? Then I have to try. Ellis, I don't know what else to do."

It was my way of making peace. I wasn't going to apologize for anything I'd said. The anger had gone out of Ellis. He was only looking at the ground, miserable.

"Now you know my secret," I said softly. I wanted to move on, erase the anger between us. "It's only fair if you tell me yours. Remember?"

Ellis shook his head, laughed ruefully under his breath, looking embarrassed.

"What is it?" I asked, suddenly not sure I wanted to know.

He looked away as he explained. "Lyla was the one who wanted me to save that money. Isn't that something? She wanted me to buy her a ring."

The words felt like ice, pouring down my throat.

"Well maybe she'll marry you without it," I said flatly. "Why don't you ask her?"

He reached for my hand again. "Are you crazy, Cathy? She knows how I feel about you. You walked in on us, remember? She guessed that day. It's over with her."

I picked a peeling piece of wood from the bunkhouse wall, breathless.

"But you like her."

"She's fine. She's great. Lyla's *really* great." He blew out a frustrated breath, looking around in annoyance. "But I *love* you, Cathy. There's not room for two."

I couldn't look at him. There were too many feelings all at once.

"Will you please look at me?" he said.

I didn't want to, but I met his eyes.

"Would you leave here with me?" I asked. "If you're right about the Electric . . . if Beezie doesn't get better . . ."

Despite what he's been saying as long as I've known him, about loving where he's landed, I expected at that moment for him to say yes. I could see how much he wanted to close the distance between us, knock it out of the way, touch me again. But his hesitation made me nervous. He looked scared, and worried.

"The dust is terrible," he said after a long spell. "I know that. But . . . the rest of the world can be terrible too. There aren't any jobs. People hate us for being poor and being from here and for taking what little jobs there are for almost no money. And on top of that we wouldn't have a house, maybe not a bed, maybe not even a roof. Beezie wouldn't be better off in San Francisco or New York. Not one bit. Here, people look out for each other."

I opened my mouth to contradict him, to say we could figure it out, but he went on.

"And then, I'm thinking about myself too. *I* don't want to spend my life surrounded by strangers. I don't think I can go back to being homeless again, or anonymous, I can't stand the thought of giving up this place. I only really started living when I came here. I don't think I could handle that uncertainty again."

"You sound like Mama."

"Well, I agree with her." He seemed to be considering his next words, like he was unsure whether he should say them or not. "And, Cathy, for all your talk, I don't think, deep down, you could go either. I think leaving here would hurt you more than you know."

All of my impassioned protests died in my throat. "I only want what's right for Beezie," I finally said. I listened to him breathing, sinking inside.

"I do too," he said.

It's keeping me from sleep tonight, wondering if he's right about me and I've never had the courage I thought I did. I always thought that if I didn't have so much holding me back, I could roam the world.

With any luck, the miraculous power of the Electric is flooding Beezie as I write this, and I won't have to choose.

JULY 11, 1934

Happiness and restlessness and fear . . . that's all these days are, one always right behind the next. I'm desperate, always desperate, to be in Ellis's room, to have some part of me touching some part of him, even if it's a finger against his wrist, even if it's my heel on the top of his ankle. It's a thread of life running through this dead place. Last night I couldn't sleep for knowing he was so close by, for worrying about Beezie, for the heat.

We received a letter from the Chiltons when we went into town today, before a duster blew up that kept us indoors all this evening. They are in San Francisco, homeless and living in a camp.

In San Francisco, they wrote, *we disappear.*

And then they shared with us the terrible news. Even weeks after leaving and breathing the clean air, their youngest child, Lizzie, has died from dust pneumonia.

JULY 17, 1934

Things are strange, it's like the feeling we get before a storm rolls up. There's so much silence in the house. Ellis brings in our groceries, he helps me carry the washtub back and forth to the well, he reaches for my hand and I reach for his and that's all for now.

Tuesday was a bad day for Beezie, who had a terrible attack. One minute everything was fine and the house was silent and the next she was calling in panic for Mama from her room saying that she couldn't breathe. The doctor came and again urged us to consider leaving.

Mama paces and looks out the windows and barely does any work. What is there to do anymore? No crops to harvest, our clothes are getting too thin and worn out to wash. There's always dust to sweep, but it will always be there.

JULY 24, 1934

It's been a week since I last wrote. Beezie knows we are in on a secret, and she keeps giving me meaningful, wide-eyed glances, and whispering, "When do I get better?" Mama sees her mincing around and assumes it's just her being her usual, dramatic self.

Her coughing gets worse every day instead of better. And I'm beginning to think that while it's true we are in on a secret, it's not the one that Beezie thinks. The secret is that I don't think the Electric has worked at all, and I don't know if I ever truly thought it would.

JULY 29, 1934

Yesterday morning was so breezy and bright and lovely, we could never have guessed what was coming. Mama and I were out enjoying the weather, our faces up to the sun, and Ellis was pumping water as best he could while a baseball game echoed from his wireless. Beezie was halfway between him and us, drawing in the dirt with sticks.

Mama had just said to me, "You know, the weather is so fine.

Maybe I'll go for a walk." She crossed the grass to Galapagos and gave her a nice long scratch on the neck and then walked off down the drive. I watched her, worried. It wasn't like her to stroll as if she didn't have a care in the world.

I kept thinking, *Get up and sweep*, and was trying to will myself into it when a small flock of blackbirds crossed the sky. I was thinking it was unusual to see so many, when a bigger, thicker flock came squawking across the horizon. I'd just looked across the yard at Ellis, and he at me, when his radio blared out, crackled, and died.

Something wobbled inside me.

Now the sky was full of birds, flying in our direction, veering a little to the left, a little to the right in waves.

When I saw the storm itself, moving in behind them, I didn't recognize it. I thought illogically that it was a mountain range—that maybe it had gotten clear enough to see all the way to Colorado.

But it was growing and moving. A sickness clutched at my stomach. It wasn't a storm but a wall coming toward us.

I could see Mama's figure for a moment between the trees, very small, and I yelled for her, but she didn't hear me. She was facing away from the incoming disaster, unaware.

The wind was already pulling at my skirt by then. Suddenly Ellis and I were both moving, running toward Beezie. I grabbed her by the armpits just as we reached each other and turned for the bunkhouse. The wind had picked up so strongly it knocked me over, and I shoved Beezie toward Ellis.

He clutched her as I made my way behind him.

We burst through the door just as the light went dim, the dust blocking the sun so thickly I couldn't see two feet in front of me.

We huddled into a corner. I held the bottom of my skirt over Beezie's nose and mouth and told her it was going to be okay. Ellis had his arms around both of us, as if he could shield us from the gritty air. My eyes and throat burned.

Around us the roof and walls moaned. I just knew that any minute they could collapse and crush us to death, or that we'd suffocate on the dust blowing through the seams in the walls.

"The world is ending!" Beezie shrieked, and it felt like a terrible thing, that nature could allow someone so small and helpless to feel so much fear. A helpless rage at God rose up with my panic.

The minutes passed, and the storm only blew harder.

When the light returned, a few minutes later, it came fast and sudden. The wind fell, and it was like someone had pulled a shade off the sun. We stood slowly.

I walked to the door and peered outside, then opened it a crack when Ellis came up behind me, touching my arm. I gasped.

We stepped out into a new world. It may as well have been the surface of the moon. The fences were gone, buried. Mama's truck was gone, buried. The house still stood, but the porch was buried too.

We shielded our eyes from the sun and looked down the drive, dumbfounded.

Dirt up to its waist, a figure was stumbling toward us.

Mama was making her way home.

JULY 30, THREE IN THE MORNING

I haven't slept. The static is so heavy in the air I can see it weaving along the fence outside, an eerie, crackling blue light. It feels like the earth has shifted under my feet, even more than it did in the storm.

Late last night, as I was writing my last entry, Mama knocked on my door, standing with a bundle of something in her arms, all wrapped in fabric. She held it so gently and carefully that at first I thought she was carrying a porcelain doll.

She walked in and sat on my bed and motioned for me to sit beside her. She looked pained as she tried to speak.

She took a deep breath, kneaded the bundle in her arms nervously.

"Yesterday . . . I thought I might not make it back home." She swallowed hard. "For the first time, I thought I'd never see you and Beezie again. And of all the terrible things I was feeling, I regretted most that you would never see these."

She unwrapped the bundle and laid it down on the bed between us—it was a pile of letters, wrinkled and worn and all in their envelopes.

"These will tell you some things about me," she said. "And about you."

She handed them to me, and I laid my hand on them in wonder and surprise and fear, because of Mama's expression. I sorted through them gently, all addressed from *Lenore Allstock, Forest Row, England.*

Mama cleared her throat and couldn't meet my eyes. "You can ask me about them, if you want. After you're finished. It's a gift I should have given you long ago," she said, pulling her hand away stiffly. "But it's a painful gift. And I'm"—she sucked in a breath—"I'm so sorry for that."

And now here I am, hours later. I've unwrapped Mama's painful gift.

Just after I finished, I trudged through the thick drifts of dust in the yard to Ellis's bunkhouse. I climbed into his bed and pulled the covers around both of us. I kissed him awake. Groggy, he tried to hold me at length to look at me, but I was insistent, kissing him until he softened his grip and gave in. His hands trembled on my arms.

"Cathy." He leaned his forehead against mine, ran his nose down the side of my neck. "What's gotten into you?"

I wanted to tell him, but I also wanted to hold the secret of Mama's letters to myself for a while longer. "Come with me," I whispered, against his cheek. "We have to go." He pulled his head back to look at me, kissed me on the lips, still groggy. "I can't make it through another storm," I said. "Beezie can't make it through another storm."

His eyes glittered in the dark as he studied me. He swallowed hard, and his voice was uneven when he spoke again. "I could never go. Going is a mistake. Cathy," he said, propping himself up, more and more alert. "We'll take Beezie to a different doctor. We'll figure out something better to cover the cracks in the house, so the dust won't get in." He swallowed nervously. "Don't pin your hopes on something out there that doesn't exist," he said, "or some ball of light or anything else. Pin them on me."

I didn't reply. I laid my head against him. His heart was pounding fast inside his chest. We lay there in the dark, and my mind kept racing. *If I don't go now,* I kept thinking, *I never will.*

I stayed there till his heart slowed and his breathing grew even. After a while he fell asleep, but my heart kept pounding. I slipped away.

Back in my room now, and I still can't shake the feeling I could leave tonight. I thought if I wrote it down it could help me choose, but it only stirs up my confusion more. Dawn is still a long way off, and there'd be time to go before Mama woke. Nobody would stop us.

All this time I've lived in Canaan, even at the darkest moments and even when I've disagreed with her, I've always believed in Mama's word, and that what she wants is what we want, and that we all belong to each other.

But it isn't true.

LENORE

PART 1

MARCH 2, 1919

Dear Beth, you can't imagine how you've shocked me!

I walked into the foyer yesterday after work, fingers stained with ink, hair in all directions, and found—sitting on the mantel by the door—your letter. It may as well have been Bluebeard's treasure, I was so surprised to see it—it's been so many weeks since I heard from you. And then I read what was inside.

You! Engaged!

I nearly fell off my feet.

Who is this man who's swept you off your feet so unexpectedly? You barely say anything about him. I'm thrilled of course, but I need more. What does he do? Where will you live?

You asked me to tell you how I'm doing. Everyone says remarkably well, given the circumstances.

Mother says the best cure for grief is to keep busy. I wish she'd take her own advice. I avoid them all as much as I can: Hubert and Gordon in black suits all the time, Vera and Ruth moping around the garden, Lawrence riding Star around the estate like the fourth horseman of the apocalypse. All any of them talks about is TeddyTeddyTeddy.

Only Father and I have stayed sane. We go off to work together and walk home together, and Teddy never comes up. Though Father *has* gone and bought the biggest memorial stone you've ever seen, to replace the one we had on the grave temporarily. Hubert says it cost a fortune, but I suppose we made so much money in the war that it doesn't matter. Remember how we used to be rich? Now we're ten times that.

Will the suffocating gloom ever lift from this house, Beth? I feel like Rapunzel, locked up in my tower by a witch, only the witch is everyone's sadness. I know if you were here, you'd save me. Without you, I'm trying to save myself and doing a poor job of it. The house is a tomb, and I am buried inside.

Compared to so many people, we've had it easy. (Mrs. Douglas lost all three sons. All of them, Beth!) Vera says that kind of logic doesn't matter. She says that since Teddy was closer to me than anyone, I should be feeling the loss the most. But I refuse to let the sadness sink me like it's sunk them.

The only thing, and I'll admit this only to you, is that I don't sleep well. And every once in a while I feel like I'm not myself. Things like: I look at my own hand and can't believe it's attached to my wrist. Or I sometimes feel like everything I see happening around me is a film instead of real life.

Otherwise, life is slowly returning to normal in Forest Row. There are things to buy in the shops now, and plenty of food, though not as much as before the war. I do payroll and administrative work at the factory, and being the boss's daughter pays well, which means saving money for my ticket to America. (I haven't given up the idea, Beth!) You'd laugh, watching me take orders. You always said I was good at giving them.

I've started taking long walks again. The other day I went looking for our Cave of the Cup—where you used to tell me the Holy Grail was buried, remember? But it must have grown over with thorn bushes because I couldn't find the way in.

I kept following the creek until long after I knew I must have passed the opening and I kept going and going. I never found it, but I did find something that took me by surprise.

It's a stone house—or what's left of one. And it's *old*: stone floors and stone walls, half crumbled in. A collapsed stick roof. I can't tell how recently, but it's clearly abandoned now. It's shrouded in bushes, which is why you and I and Teddy must have missed it all these years on our walks.

I went in, pushing the cobwebs and branches out of my way. There was an old table, half standing, and a bowl and a plate set as if some person years ago had just gotten up and left right before dinner. There was a mantel above the fireplace, still intact, chimney and all.

If we were still little, we'd say it was haunted by the ghosts of dead Germans and claim it for our hideout (Teddy would sneak around and throw things in through the window to scare us). Now it's just an empty house.

As you can tell, there isn't much to do. At first when someone dies, you feel so surrounded by everyone telling you how sorry they are. Then that all fades away and you're left—not with all that noise and activity anymore—but just with one less person in your life than you used to have.

Don't worry, Beth, when I finally make it to you in New York, I'll be the girl you remember. I won't let the war and everything that went with it crumple me up. I'll live next door to you wherever you end up, and help with all your babies when you have them. It won't be quite what we used to picture as children, where we get married in a double wedding to famous actor brothers, but it'll be good enough. I promise you, I won't change.

P.S. Here's the book I promised you, *Grimm's Fairy Tales*, the one we scribbled all over, though I'm a little nervous putting something so sentimental in the mail in case it sinks on the way over. Also just to prove we're grown-ups, I'm sending *Dubliners*, though I only half understood it.

P.P.S. Did I ever tell you that sometimes I look east and imagine that, if there were no trees and no curve on the Earth, I'd be able to see you? Do you ever do silly things like that?

Send more news when you can.

MARCH 16, 1919

Dear Beth,

I was so excited to get your letter! I can't believe you're moving to Kansas. People say you can plant anything in the ground in the American West and it grows. I have to admit, I never saw you as a farmer or a farmer's wife, but I'm very happy for you.

There's a parade in town today, to remember the soldiers. I decided to stay home . . . for one because I have something strange to tell you, and for another because I can't take another parade where everything centers on the dead and we all act as though we may as well be dead too, even though we're not.

On Sunday we had several families from around the village over for a dinner. Mother said it'd been too long since we'd all gotten together, but really I think she sees any gathering as a chance to marry us off. Matchmaking is the only thing that stirs her to life anymore. Maybe if we were all permanently out of the house, she wouldn't have to get dressed in the morning. She wouldn't have to breathe. She could lie down at Teddy's headstone and never get up.

The boy she picked out for me (for some reason, she focuses mostly on *me*) was too boring to even write much about. He's a coward, for one thing. He watched all his friends join up before he finally got conscripted when boys like Teddy were joining up first thing. And he was so unforgivably serious: *I'msorryforyourloss this and that.*

My face hurt from pretending to be interested while shooting annoyed glances at Mother, who didn't notice. (It's like she wants someone to come along and plug a hole inside me. She doesn't see that there is no hole.) She says marriage and motherhood is everything. "I nearly died giving birth to Gordon," she likes to say, "but it was worth it! Then of course I went on to have five more children!"

The conversation went on eternally. People kept arriving, and it got so stuffy and hot in the house, and I was so tired of *Mr. Sorryforyourloss* that I walked out the back door to get some air, and then just set off across the field. I went all the way to the edge of the woods to the fence that marks off our land, and then I stood there and tried to catch my breath for a minute.

Then, on impulse, I doubled back to the housekeeper's shed for a broom, and then climbed over the fence with it, into the woods, and walked all the way back to the abandoned cottage.

Once I got there I began to sweep. It was like something had taken me over, and all I wanted at that moment was to get the place as clean as possible. I swept out every leaf, every piece of dirt that had accumulated in the corners for God knows how many years. By the time I was finished, the house was still broken, but it was spotlessly broken.

I didn't trail home until after the dinner was over and all the guests were gone. No one seemed to have noticed: Vera was sitting on the sofa braiding Ruth's hair (with black ribbon, of course), and Hubert was in the library, no doubt reading depressing poetry. This is another thing about losing Teddy. When he was alive he was just one of us. Now that he's gone, he's the only one anyone thinks about.

Anyway, over the past few days I've been to the cottage several times to clear out more debris from the crevices in the walls, brought down some old pillows and jars and things Mother won't miss to make it comfortable, and propped up the old table with some bricks that were scattered close by in the ivy.

I suppose you'll tell me I've lost my mind. I don't know what to say except that being there and fixing things makes me feel awake, and it's the only place to be truly alone. Though, as stupid as it sounds, I mostly just sit at this old table (where I am now!) and have imaginary conversations with you. I think of this place as ours. And maybe that's the strangest part.

Well, no, that's not quite right. The strangest part is that every once in a while, when I'm home sitting up in my window where I have a good view of the woods, I swear I can see smoke wafting up from this spot in the trees. So maybe I am losing my mind after all.

I've been doing some counting. Remember how after I fell off the barn roof that one summer I was always getting hurt, I liked to count my broken bones? The clavicle, the sacrum, the tiny bones in the wrist—going over them again and again to pass the weeks I spent in bed recovering? Now I count time.

It's been three years and eleven months since they sank the *Lusitania* and a year and ten months since the first zeppelin bombed London. It's been four years and thirteen days since you left Forest Row, and by my calculations it will be four more months before I can save up the money to see you again.

All I do is work and read. Work is fine, though none of the workers seem to like me much. It's only my first year and I'm only seventeen, but I make more money than most of them, and sometimes I suspect they know it.

This time I'm enclosing *Ethan Frome.* Ruth bought it for me. It's very tragic.

Love, Lenore

APRIL 1, 1919

Dear Beth,

I can barely hear myself think, my heart is beating so hard as I think about what to write. We're all going to a workers' picnic at the factory, and Vera and Ruth are running up and down the hall looking for things to wear. I'm not sure how much I'll be able to get down before I have to run, but something so startling happened last night that I can't keep it in. I'll need to explain what led up to it, which is also confusing in its own way.

The new cinema opened last night, only three train stops and we're there. I won at drawing straws so Mother took me as her date. The theme is Arabian Nights. It's full of stars and spires—the kind of thing we would have fainted over when we were little. (Kindly, you would have given me the middle seat. I would have made you give me half your candy.)

In actuality it was so lovely and perfect, but I have to admit that the whole thing felt a bit flat, like there was no sparkle to any of it. I sat there thinking how the stage lights are just chemical reactions and not magical objects like they might have seemed a few years ago. I kept looking around at all the faces turned so raptly to the screen and wished I could be as absorbed as they were. Though it makes no sense, I always find myself looking for Teddy among crowds—for that aggressive, spiky brown hair of his and that smirk that used to annoy me. It's a stupid habit, but I can't seem to break it.

A one-armed boy winked at me from the row ahead of us (if you toss a pebble in Forest Row you're going to hit a one-armed boy). I gave him a look to say *not a chance.* Not because of the lack of limbs, but because I feel like these boys are always asking something like comfort from me, even if it's just with their eyes. Mother cried through most of the film even though it was a comedy. Then we came home and went to bed. Everything was normal.

So I couldn't say why some time around midnight, I woke in a panic. My heart was beating fast like I'd been sprinting. And I couldn't calm down. I kept remembering—of all things—how Teddy once saved my pet duck from becoming dinner by hiding him in his room—how he called me in in a whisper and showed me, and said, "He'll live to quack another day." I couldn't get it out of my head.

Finally, I snuck downstairs and pulled on my wool jumper and boots and walked out across the field in the moonlight and the drizzle, and down to the creek and wound my way to the cottage because it was the only place I could think of to get away from myself.

I was—I admit—a little afraid of running into something scary in the dark, but I was more afraid of staying in my room and having my heart beat out of my chest. It smelled like dew and grass and rain, and I watched the ground for grass snakes as I walked.

Now that I think about it, I've ignored the signs all along. The bowl set neatly on the table. The smoke from the chimney, the half-mended roof.

I burst inside without a thought, tried to light the candles but my hands were shaking. It was like there was some invisible thread between Teddy saving my duck all those years ago and the ground underneath me, the cells of my skin and my shaking hands. At last I gave up and sank down on the floor against the wall and tried to catch my breath. A moan escaped from my lips, a thing inside that had nowhere else to go but out. I held my breath for a moment, and was surprised to find I could still hear myself wheezing. But, Beth, I'm sure you can guess by now that the wheezing wasn't mine.

Mother is outside beating the door down. Sorry to leave you—I'll have to finish when I get back.

LATER—

It's late, too late to write really, but I need to tell you the rest before I go to sleep. You know how I like to finish things.

I was squatting there in the cottage, frozen in fear. All sorts of terrifying possibilities were flashing through my mind: everything from Germans who hadn't heard all year that the war was over . . . to a creature from one of our fairy tales: a witch or the troll under the bridge. But as my eyes adjusted to the light I could see that there was a figure against the far wall cowering from *me.*

And in that moment, my humiliation outstripped my fear. I tried to compose myself.

"Who's there?" I called out.

A long pause. I was beginning to think there'd be no answer when a voice snaked out of the darkness. "Kaiser Wilhelm." A male, English voice, amused but a little blurry, like he had marbles in his mouth.

There was a long silence, a shifting. I could hear him scratching at his hair, his cheeks, furiously.

I stood. My hands were steady now. I grabbed the matches from where I'd left them and lit the candle in one try.

I moved to cast the light toward him, and the flames leapt dimly over his shape. As his face emerged from the shadows, I sucked in my breath. He was missing an ear, and his left cheek looked *drippy*, like candle wax.

Beth, I've seen other men horribly wounded by the war, and I know how you're supposed to act: don't flinch but also don't pretend, make eye contact, shake hands. I know all that, but I've never seen a person look so far from being a person.

"Lenore Allstock," I said, thrusting out my hand, but flinching all the same when he stretched up from the floor and let his fingers touch mine.

"Pleasure," he said, his voice deep and polite, but with a hint of laughter in it, as he unraveled himself to his full height, either not noticing my flinch or pretending not to. He was enormously tall, at least two feet taller than Teddy. A giant.

Looking past him, I could see a bedroll in a corner where he must have been lying until I came in, and a rucksack.

"You've been sleeping here?" I asked.

"For a couple of weeks."

"I've never seen you . . ."

"I only spend the nights, and evenings. Also, I clear out when

I hear you coming. There's plenty of time. You walk like a bear."

I felt my whole body stiffen. I was suddenly ready to defend that little dingy room to the death. "You're trespassing."

"Well . . . ," he said with hesitation. "Clearly it's a well-loved and indispensable piece of the estate."

He studied me. His face was so ruined I couldn't tell if he was being menacing or teasing or both.

"Look, Miss Allstock, is it? I like staying here." He pointed to the roof; I followed his gaze up to where I saw now, even in the dim light, he'd done some patching. "I've worked hard to improve it. Maybe we could work something out? Unless you plan on more of these nocturnal visits, we'd never even have to cross paths." He leaned against the wall and put his hands in his pockets. "I spend the whole day out hounding. I don't usually come back until the evenings. I could make a point of that."

"Hounding?"

He sighed and rubbed at his ruined face. "Fossil hunting. That's how I found this place. I was out hounding and it seemed . . . perfect."

I watched him. "I'm not sure . . ."

"In the stream here, all sorts of fossils. Old bird bones, fish skeletons, things like that, frozen in time."

I held up my hand, impatient. "I'm not worried about the bird bones. I just don't know why I should let you stay."

He gestured casually to his face. "Is it enough to say I need to be away from the city for a while? And that you should take pity on a poor war hero?" His voice cracked on the last words, and it made me realize he was younger than I'd thought he was. His size had misled me.

I studied him skeptically.

"Look." He became suddenly serious, his voice dropping an octave. "In London, people stare. In the woods . . ." He nodded out toward the darkness. "The raccoons don't care if I'm missing my face. Know what I mean? I need a break. Isn't that why *you* come here? You need a break?"

I felt my face flush, and shook my head to contradict him.

"We all need a break," he said, more to himself than to me.

I stood there uncertainly for a few moments longer. On one hand, I wanted to keep everything as I'd thought it had been: all mine. On the other, how could I refuse him?

"So you'll let me stay?" he said, turning a confident smile on me or at least half a one. "We'll share?"

I laid my candlesticks on the table and nodded. "For now I guess that's all right," I said. "But it's *my* place, in the end. Don't forget that."

He nodded and then winced.

"Are you all right?"

"Yes," he said impatiently. "Of course. Just one more thing . . . can you please not mention to anyone that I'm here? I don't want people showing up with baskets of buns. I just want to be alone."

I nodded. I was about to leave and was moving toward the door, but I back-stepped when I saw him clasping his hands together suddenly and sharply in pain. A shudder passed through him and then he straightened again and struck a careless pose with his hand at the window.

"Can I get you anything?" I asked. "Do you have any money? There's a chemist in town. I could get you some . . ."

"Oh, I go back home for supplies. My family has a good doctor, plenty of money."

"Are you sure?" I asked.

He looked me up and down and smiled ruefully. "Thank you. I just need peace."

And that was it. I haven't seen him since.

I've decided to stay true to my word and not tell a soul about him, even though he could be a thief or a murderer or both.

I already know he's a liar, because if he's from a wealthy London family why are his clothes all frayed and old? And if he's a wounded veteran, why is he hiding in a cottage in Forest Row instead of being treated in the city like the war hero he is?

My hand hurts because I wrote that all in a rush. It's nearing midnight, and I can hear someone sniffling and crying quietly all the way down the hall but I don't know who it is. I love my family, but sometimes I think they're all so pathetic, awful as it is to admit. My eyelids are drooping.

Good night, Beth.

No books to send with this post.

Your friend, Lenore

APRIL 11, 1919

Beth,

Just a brief note, as the post is about to leave, and I feel like this morning you're especially far away. I haven't heard from you in weeks, and I think maybe you must be on a honeymoon. Could it be true that you are married by now, as you said you'd be? I'm happy for you, if so. It's just that I woke with an emptiness in my chest, coming out of a dream of you, me, and Teddy. We were eleven and twelve—the age we were just before you left—and sitting on the lawn in front of the house, when a German zeppelin rose right behind us and over us and the house like the moon, flying over Forest Row. It was headed to London to drop bombs.

We couldn't help thinking how beautiful it was, like it was sent from heaven. And then I realized that it wasn't sent from heaven but from the war, and even though it was already past us I kept squeezing the grass underneath my legs, saying that I wouldn't let the ground go. And then I woke up. I tried as hard as I could to fall back asleep and find you both again, but I couldn't.

I'm a sleepwalker today. Do you think it was God talking to me? You've always been more of a believer than me, Beth! Maybe you can put in a good word for me.

In case you're wondering, I've been back to the cottage many times but seen no sign of the giant (I never got his name) at all. He never even leaves his rucksack behind. I wonder if maybe he's left altogether or if he's just good at erasing himself.

I still imagine, whenever I'm there, that you are too. Talking to you in my head is like putting my brain through the laundry. You tell me I've impressed you with how strong I am to move on with life like I have. You point out what I could do better, like you used to.

Speaking of which, Douglas Fairbanks is my new soul mate. Do you think I have a chance? He's so good looking I don't think I'd mind *what* kind of personality he has.

APRIL 22, 1919

Dear Beth,

Over a month and no letter from you, and I'm wondering if something is wrong? We officially put away the mourning today—the black cloth around the bureau in the hall, the mourning brooch mounted in front of Teddy's photo, and everyone's gotten out of their black clothes. I'm relieved. And busy. The whole town is busy.

London is gearing up for the Fair of Lights, and Mother's invited a lecturer to the town hall to speak to everyone about the innovations of industry and the productivity of mechanized labor. The lecturer is a friend of Father's and has been advising him on reconfiguring the factory to run more efficiently. Some of the workers are upset about it; many of them will be working longer hours and some talk about the increased soot in the air. It's all boring except to Father, whose eyes brighten with enthusiasm whenever the word *efficiency* comes into play.

I'm the organizer—getting the hall ready, getting the train schedules lined up for visitors. It's draining at times. Someone rubbed Father's shoes in manure last week when he'd taken them off outside the factory door to change into work boots. It's related to either labor or contamination of the river or both. He just wiped them off with his handkerchief and went on as if nothing had happened. He's an honest man, at the bottom of everything.

I hadn't had a moment to get down to the cottage until yesterday, and I guess that, with so much time passing between my visits, the little improvements the giant has made have added up (he's not gone after all). He's continued rebuilding the roof, though it's hard to imagine it ever being finished.

I made two trips to the house to bring some things back—a small Union Jack that I poached from Teddy's grave (sacrilege!) and next to it, a small stack of magazines and pillows. This morning when I returned with candlesticks (Mother has six sets), he'd added some things too: a jar of wild roses, several small rocks, a snail shell, and another shell that I didn't recognize.

Clearly the giant has no interest in being friends, and neither do I. But it's nice to be alone and yet have this feeling of having company at the same time.

P.S. I was just writing that last part when I heard a noise and got up to see what it was. Forget what I just wrote. I think I was wrong.

APRIL 23, 1919

Dear Beth,

I'm lying in bed, propped on my pillows. Downstairs the house is coming alive—pots and pans being banged around in the kitchen. A crack of bright light is falling on me through the curtain.

Last night I was writing to you (letter enclosed with this one) after the rest of the family had gone to sleep. I could hear Ruth and Vera in their room talking and then settling down, and Gordon rattling around with some school project he's building downstairs. I was sitting in the window writing the last words when an orange flicker caught the corner of my eye, and I looked out onto the lawn to see an invisible hand waving a cigarette. It was a cloudy, dark night, but as the cigarette moved the hand holding it and the rest of its owner came into view: the giant. I pulled on my robe and tiptoed downstairs and out onto the lawn. He was waiting by the bottom stair, his misshapen form looming at me from the shadows.

"What's wrong?" I asked, alarmed. "Is everything all right?"

"Everything's fine," he said, wincing. "I was just wondering if you'd like to come over for dinner."

I looked up at the moon. "It's almost ten o'clock."

"Yes."

"I already ate."

He just stood silently, waiting.

"I thought you wanted to get *away* from people."

He shrugged. "I thought I didn't smoke either." He began to

tremble, let out a hiss, and sank down onto the grass. "To be honest, I just need to take my mind off how much everything hurts."

I let out a slow breath and looked at the overcast sky, wide awake now.

"All right. I just have to sign off on a letter. What'll I bring?"

Down at the cottage, he had a bottle of wine waiting but no glasses. I'd raided the kitchen for rolls and cold chicken and half a wheel of cheese, but I hadn't thought of that.

"We'll have to drink from the bottle," he said. And we did.

I was suddenly starving, and we talked between mouthfuls. He asked me about my parents, the factory, my job. He told me he grew up in Knightsbridge and—his eyes shifting away from mine—that his parents, famous naturalists who work at the British Museum, are out of the country on some kind of important expedition. I don't mind that I don't believe him. Mostly, the pain he was in was distracting to both of us. When he wasn't eating, he kept his arms wrapped around his chest like he was trying to hold himself together.

"Where did you fight?" I asked.

"Sensitive subject," he said, "don't you think? Given that I left my ear there?"

"What's your name?" I changed tack, embarrassed.

He smiled at that. "James."

He stood to light the fire but couldn't strike a match with his thick, scarred fingers. He made a fist and pounded it on the mantel in annoyance. I sat looking on uncertainly until he shot a glare at me. "Wouldn't want to help a bloke?"

As I lit the kindling he stomped around the cottage whistling "God Save the King" impatiently while I got everything going. Even his whistling has sarcasm in it.

His lips are so damaged that he can't drink anything without some of it dribbling out the side of his mouth. I think he was feeling self-conscious, because he kept letting out loud, angry sighs.

"Can I help?" I asked.

"Just pretend you don't notice," he retorted.

"Well, make up your mind," I said. "Do you want me to offer to help or do you want me to pretend I don't notice?"

He smiled again, and this time it gave me this sudden glimpse of what his face used to look like. At the same time, it was as if there was a little bit of air let out between us with all the bluntness, and things became more comfortable.

We got a little drunk. I didn't ask him any more about the war, and he didn't ask me about my strange breakdown the first and last time we'd been in the cottage together. I told him how Mother is trying to marry me off. He told me more about fossil collecting, which bored me to tears.

And we talked about you. He initiated it.

"Now, Allstock," he said, after we'd finished our last bites.

"Lenore," I said.

"Allstock." He leaned back against the wall looking at me seriously and intensely. "I've got a personal question for you, since we're asking those kinds of questions. Who's your invisible friend? The place settings? The putting flowers out for someone who never shows up? Who died?"

I stared down at my plate in the flickering of the fire, embarrassed again, but not as much as before.

"I have a friend in America," I said finally. "I just imagine she's here."

Because he seemed to be waiting for more, and no one ever asks me about you, I told him how we grew up together, how when war was brewing your parents took you to America to get you out of harm's way. How I'm planning to follow you there so we can be lifelong neighbors.

He smiled. "And how long has she been gone?" he asked.

"Since just before the *Lusitania*," I said.

"So since we were kids."

I nodded.

"So she *is* your imaginary friend."

I looked at him, annoyed.

"Well, Allstock . . ."

"Lenore."

"I'm sure you've changed so much—with everything that's happened, and just . . . getting older," he said. "And her too. It's inevitable that you'd both be completely different now. It's likely that if you met again, you wouldn't like each other. So what's the point of having imaginary tea together?"

"I haven't changed," I said.

His eyes flickered with doubt. "They've been in mourning at

your house," he said. "Who died? Your father?"

"My brother. And please shut up with that look." I pushed myself back, away from him.

"I can't stand sad looks either, believe me." He cupped his hands on either side of his lips and lifted them in a pretend smile. "That better? Sorry, but my lips got bombed into a permanent frown."

I smiled, despite myself. There was something about the way he treated the most horrific things that made me feel like I could breathe.

"What was your brother like?" he asked lightly. As if he were asking *Do you have plans Saturday?* or *How is the pie?*

I surprised myself by answering honestly. "He was closest to me in age, out of all of us," I said. "People always called us 'the twins.' He always stood up for me. And teased me. But on the important things, he always stood up for me."

"You've lost your almost-twin," he said, thrusting the almost-empty wine bottle into my hands. "Well, you deserve the last drink then."

I thought how we were treading in a dangerous place. To not enrage me about Teddy, one has to walk a thin line of comprehension without pity. I wanted to pull away from the subject, and uncharitably, it seemed like a good moment to catch James off guard. "When do your parents get back from their expedition?" I asked.

He did look momentarily caught.

"They're on their way back now," he asserted after a moment, gazing everywhere but at my face (though to be fair, that's generally the way he talks).

I wonder if he thinks he has to pretend to come from money because he assumes I do. And I want so much to know his real story. But I didn't push it. It's not that I feel sorry for him—though it's sad to see how he thinks about his face all the time. It's clear in the way he rubs at it, runs his hands over his ear and his half-ear as if he can't believe their shape, and touches his lips self-consciously.

"You're no good at pretending you don't notice," he finally said as I watched him. "Did anyone ever tell you that?"

I shook my head.

"Maybe you should wear a fake mustache to distract people," I offered.

He let out a loud booming laugh, which startled me enough to make me laugh too. I think it was the first time I've laughed in months.

"Well, it's been nice," he said, tapping his lips. "And I think I haven't thought about how bad my body feels for about an hour. Maybe it's the wine."

I stood to go, knowing it was my cue.

We said good-bye at the door.

I haven't seen him since. At least I didn't flinch again when we shook hands good-bye.

All right, Beth, I know what you're thinking. You're thinking this is just like one of our books, like *Beauty and the Beast.* But

I'm too superficial and selfish to be Beauty, and he's not going to turn back into a handsome prince like the Beast. Anyway, when I meet my soul mate he won't be sarcastic and he'll always call me by my first name.

But to put your mind even further to rest, James told me something else: he's engaged to a girl in London who is very beautiful. I didn't believe it until he showed me her photo, which he keeps in his rucksack with whatever other few things he's unable to live without.

It makes me relieved for him, and a little for myself. That there doesn't have to be that question lingering over us. And we can really be actual friends.

MAY 1, 1919

Dear Beth,

I hope there's nothing wrong and that you're just too deliriously happy and preoccupied to write. I'm going to keep writing to you, because I assume you want to hear about my exciting life here where every day is just about the same.

The only interesting thing, as usual, is the cottage and James the Giant.

For a month or so after I last wrote, given that we run on different times and in different worlds, I didn't see him at all. But those weeks we *did* communicate through things we left for each other: jars of honey, bird bones, little rocks he's broken in half—quartz and pyrite. I left him a note telling him I hoped he was feeling better, and he left me a note saying he hoped I was going on lots of dates like Mother wants me to.

Finally, last Saturday my parents were away for a conference on machinery. So bright and early, I got up and strolled down across the pasture to the woods to check in on him.

James was in the clearing, sawing sticks for the roof.

"Is this really what you do with all your time?" I asked.

He let out a laugh. "It occupies my mind," he said, straightening up and letting his saw drop onto the ground. (There are things I hadn't noticed about him at night—the veins of crinkled skin stretching across his face and down his neck look like the roots of an old, gnarled tree.)

"What's new, Allstock?" he asked, straightening up and walking toward me as he shoved his hands in his pockets. I told him how two people in town have the Spanish flu but are recovering, and that I'd been to the cinema twice, but only with Hubert and Gordon.

"Mostly anything anyone talks about is the Fair of Lights," I added.

"Are you going?" he asked.

"Everyone's going." I picked up one of the sticks he'd sawed and rubbed my fingers over its rough edges carelessly. "One has to go."

"Why does *one have to go*?" he repeated.

"Well, I don't know." We were being playful, and it felt nice. The sun was sparkling and the air was soft and it felt good to be smiling with someone. "To see what there is to see. You know, ride the rides. See the magnificent inventions. Witness the miracle of industry," I repeated an advert I'd seen in the newspaper in a booming voice.

"Industry made the war," he said with a shrug. "Industry is the world's great evil."

"How ridiculous," I retorted. "People made the war."

"You need to read your newspapers, Allstock. It's all about inventing better ways to destroy things. It's about money. Welcome to the violent industrial age, Lenore. You don't even know you're in it."

"It *is* miraculous," I said finally. "And I don't care if you agree."

James was still silent and unconvinced, and because I didn't want to argue on such a beautiful day with the only person I really wanted to see, I nodded to the rocks he'd lined up on the windowsill of the cottage.

"If you're interested in finding some *real* treasures, I know where the Holy Grail is buried," I said.

He raised his eyebrows.

"Well," I offered, "at least I know a really good cave."

All along the way, James collected things—rocks of course, pieces of moss, a mushroom, a snail shell. Some things he pocketed, and some things he threw back. He held out a shell to me.

"Some snail didn't think it was worth keeping, so why should you?" I said.

He looked down at the shell, disappointed. "No reason," he said, and chucked it.

This time, because I was determined and had an extra scout at my disposal, I found the entrance that last time I couldn't find. It was grown over, just as I'd thought, but nothing that a little bush-beating didn't reveal.

Inside, the cavern is just as you'd remember it. Narrow at the opening, then widening into a big, jagged circle. We hadn't brought a candle so we just had to go by the dim light filtering into the entrance.

We sat down on a boulder at one side, next to each other, listening to the *drip, drip* of the water running somewhere nearby. James broke a stalactite off the stone ceiling sloping above us.

"Every inch takes about two hundred years to grow," he said. "Here." He handed it to me, and I turned it over in my hands. "These are more miraculous than any Grail," he went on. "They're truly ancient." I began to break it apart, piece by piece in my hands.

"Beth said she'd already found the Grail," I mused, "and put it back in here somewhere. She was always telling me things like that—that she'd run into a celebrity on the train, or found ten pounds on the street—silly things I was so jealous of. She said she couldn't remember exactly where inside the cave she'd buried it. I was surprised because Beth was scared of the dark. She was timid."

I pointed toward the small crevice shaped like a skull high in the back, above a particularly treacherous ledge. "That's where she said she thought she'd hidden it. We kept coming back, and I kept climbing up to look for it. Beth was never a climber." I leaned back against the spiny wall behind me. I ran my hands through my hair. For some reason, being in the cave reminded me of what it felt like to be in my body when I was younger, everything closer and more vivid. (Since Teddy died, I barely notice my senses at all. It's like my body is far away from the rest of me.)

"Jesus's cup . . . right here in Forest Row. How did it all end up?"

I smiled. "Badly. I broke my arm falling off the ledge. We weren't allowed back here after that."

"Must have smarted a bit."

I thought back. I remember it so clearly, Beth. I wonder if you do too.

"I wanted to cry. But I couldn't. Beth often said I did things for attention, and I think she was right. So I kept pretending to laugh. I wanted to prove her wrong. I told her it tickled.

"Anyway, the following summer the war was on. And she left. It was awful. We both cried our eyes out when we found out she was leaving. And I promised that if she stayed in America, I'd follow her. And that's what I'm planning on. That's what I'm building my life around now."

"She sounds . . ." He trailed off. "Like a character."

"Well, not around most people. She's very quiet and shy. But much kinder than I am. We both always knew that."

We sat for a while longer.

I studied him, now more seriously. "Can I ask you something?"

"Oh God. I don't know, Lenore. It's going to do with my

hideous deformity, isn't it?" He dropped his face into his hands, with a sort of laugh/cry expression.

"Sort of," I admitted. Since he seemed to be willing, I faltered on. "What did your fiancée say when she saw you the first time, after . . . ?"

He looked over at me for a long moment. "How can you possibly be comfortable asking that?" He was wry but his hands shook a little, and I felt guilty.

"I'm sorry."

"It's okay." He shook his head, put both hands on the ceiling of the cave as if he might pull himself into a chin-up, and then let go. "I was scared, you know, to see her. I almost preferred never seeing her again to having her see me like this." He tapped his hands together. "I made her wait months, till I was out of the hospital. I wanted to be on my own two feet when we met again, not in some bed, in a hospital gown. I didn't want to look like I was *completely helpless,* just *mostly helpless.* I went to her house. We picked a time. I stood on the front porch and knocked and waited, and it was the most frightening moment of my life."

"And?"

He looked up at me, then far away. "She opened the door. She looked at me for a long while. She took my face in her hands and kissed my cheek, right on one of the scars. She told me, 'You're a beautiful sight.'"

Beth, is that not the most romantic thing you've ever heard? Though I'm sure your husband's proposal was so stunningly romantic that it tops even that. Please tell me the details.

Love, Lenore

P.S. I wasn't going to write this. But I've been sitting here for almost twenty minutes now and I've decided I have to.

I need to ask if you have left me behind, Beth? Is that why you haven't written?

Maybe James the Giant is right, and you've changed more than I know.

I'm glad for you that you're going forward in life. I just hope that wherever you're going, I'm going too. But it doesn't have to be that way.

Fifty-two pounds saved (I need seventy plus money to live on once I get there), and I'm still planning to come unless I hear otherwise. I hope that I'm still invited.

Love, Lenore

MAY 15, 1919

Beth,

You can't imagine how relieved I was to get your letter. And how happy I am that everything is not only all right but rosy in your world. Your farm sounds magnificent and so does your life. Though the letter was too short and didn't give enough details. I forgive you.

You sent your letter before you got mine, and so I just want to say that you should please ignore the last postscript. It was a moment of weakness. I know you're still waiting for me and counting on me. I know you and I know us and I'm sorry that for a moment I lost my faith.

Since I last wrote I've been out on three dates with *I'msorry-foryourloss* (real name Christopher, apparently). I know what I said about him, but he's very nice and harmless and it makes Mother happy. And everyone's spirits have seemed to lift in recent weeks since the official end of mourning—we had a family game of badminton in the yard last Friday, and I even hear Vera and Hubert laughing together sometimes. It's odd, because I find that while everyone's getting better, I'm about the same.

I spent all weekend helping James with the roof. It's strange: we see each other rarely, and some days we're delighted to spend time together and laugh and joke around—especially about inappropriate things like "limbless Larries" (how James refers to the men at the convalescent home, whom Mother visits with baskets of food). Other days, I have to admit, we can't stand each other. I get in these unpredictable angry moods, and I think James gets angry too.

Sunday was one of those days. I'd come to help. The work is hard, and I have my doubts about whether repairing the roof of a house no one will ever live in is the best use of our time. James was having a lot of pain, which always makes him irritable.

He was barking orders at me to lay the sticks this way and that, as if he's any better of an architect than I am, and his loud raspy breathing was getting on my nerves even though I know that technically he can't help it and I'm an awful person for feeling that way.

I felt like taking a jab at him, so I decided to steer the conversation to his parents and why—if they're traveling all over the world doing things he also loves doing—they didn't take him with them. I wanted to fluster him and get him to be truthful for once, but he didn't seem flustered at all.

"I *did* go with them once," he answered, "when I was a little boy, for a two-year voyage. When I came back I had no social skills."

"That explains so much," I said.

"Allstock, we both know I'm charming." He was serious, and he said it so matter-of-factly it annoyed me. "Anyway, I'm going with them on the next one."

"And what does your fiancée think about your plans to leave her for the other side of the world?"

Suddenly, I knew I had him. He paused, startled, and stared up at the roof where he'd been preparing to climb. He let out a small, slow breath. "She's patient," he finally said. Then he offered a jab of his own. "What's new with you? Has your imaginary friend offered a reason for all her silences? I suppose it's hard to tell someone you're not writing to them because slowly you're forgetting them."

Long story short, I ended up telling him about when we became blood sisters. Do you remember this, Beth?

We were about eight or nine. We were both going to cut our hands, then let the blood mingle together, so we'd be related to each other forever. It was my idea as usual, because I was always the one putting us up to ridiculous things. I'd gotten a knife from the kitchen. You were supposed to cut first, but at the last moment, you got squeamish and sick to your stomach, so we didn't do it.

Then, a few weeks later, we were out one afternoon racing with Teddy on the gravel path into town, and you fell and cut your knee. And with sudden inspiration, I ran into the house and came out with a knife.

With Teddy looking on in disbelief, I sliced the knife down the center of my palm before I could let myself be afraid, and then I made you lie still so I could stick my hand onto your knee and squash all the blood in. I still remember the look on your face, though I couldn't read it. Were you put off by my crazy determination?

"Beth always said I could be bossy," I admitted to James.

"I think she must have meant fearless."

"No," I shook my head. "I'm afraid of a lot of things." He raised his eyebrows, wanting me to go on. "But I'm not a coward. That's one thing I could never be. I'd hate myself. That's why I could do it, cut my hand like that."

James considered that. "Did you ever find out why Beth lied to you about the Cup?"

It was a strange question, out of nowhere. And I don't know the answer, and it doesn't seem important.

"And what did Teddy think of the whole episode?" he went on, switching the subject back.

"He thought we were insane."

"I agree with your brother."

I smiled. It's strange, but I'm better at thinking of Teddy when I'm with James than when I'm alone. Maybe it's that I can't help Teddy (I would give anything to help him; I'd give anything to take part of his death for myself so he didn't have to be completely dead), but I *can* help James . . . make him laugh sometimes, even though we often just irritate each other.

And that's something. Though I don't know whether it makes me sad or happy or just uncomfortable. Like something is raw in my chest.

You can tell by the way he talks about his fiancée how in love he is—even the way he says her name—it's like he's holding little bird bones gently between his lips, careful not to break them. I wonder if that's the way you feel now too, now that you've found someone.

Where are you, Beth? You wrote to me, but it feels like you were absent behind the words. James says that he calls you imaginary because you're so long gone that I can make of you in my head what I want to. But he doesn't know that half the time, it seems like I'm imagining even him, even myself.

Sometimes it feels like you're the only person who is real to me anymore, even though I never see you. And it scares me that you're slipping away.

LATER—

I've just picked my pen up again and now it's the middle of the night. I need to confess something to you, Beth. I haven't been completely honest. I know what's been making me so angry.

The last few nights I haven't been able to help it, or push it away like I used to. In my mind I try to follow Teddy into those last moments. I imagine what it's like to be that afraid. I try to think what he must have been thinking, as if the one thing I can do for him now is to experience what he experienced and feel what he felt. I know you'll say this makes no sense because I can never know. But I can't control it.

And the truth is something I don't want to admit: it's been a year since Teddy died, and every day I'm strange to myself and getting stranger all the time. I think I was wrong and that I'm not Rapunzel at all, locked up and stuck away by an evil witch. I think *I am* the witch. At these times, when I lie awake and I can't stop thinking about Teddy's last moments, I'm the one who tries to put Hansel and Gretel and all the good and innocent things in the oven to burn. When I really think about Teddy, when I *really let myself think about him,* I want to eat people alive.

And now I'm up and wide awake and my parents are away and I have this whole beautiful empty house to myself, which anyone would be lucky to have. And all I can think is that James's fiancée doesn't see his scars at all, while I can't forget them. And even *he*—even my friend—seems enragingly lucky to me.

Despite his courage and all that he's given up for the greater good, he could be the one who is dead and Teddy could be alive. And then, terrible as it is to say, I would be happy.

JUNE 6, 1919

Beth,

I didn't hear from you after my last letter, and I can understand why. In this particular letter I will be sane and funny and bright.

Here's something completely lovely. James gave me a surprise.

I came home from work hoping to find a letter from you, but instead there was one from him, mixed in with all the other letters, sealed in an envelope addressed to me, and with—in the return address section—the words *The Royal Ladies' Society of Grail Seekers* and *Their Lowly Male Friends.*

I opened it with eager curiosity.

> *Surprise for you. Waiting at the cottage. Any night you can get away.*

Though I wanted to, I couldn't get away until Thursday because we had visitors. I hadn't given James any notice I was coming, but when I arrived around nine, he had candles going as if he'd been expecting me. He opened the door with a grin and said to my puzzled gaze, "You have the loudest tread known to man or beast of the forest. I've told you that."

He'd picked up a bottle of wine and poured us two glasses (we have those now), and then he led me outside and around to the side of the house. We arrived at the bottom of the ladder and stood there looking at each other dumbly.

"Here, I'll give you a leg up," he offered.

I looked up. "Onto the roof?"

He nodded.

I waved his hands away. "I know how to get up a ladder."

I climbed up ahead of him and then looked around.

"What am I looking at?"

"Keep going up."

"It'll break."

"It won't. I promise you."

I crawled out onto the threaded sticks of the roof. The moon above, as I caught sight of it above the tree line, was enormous and full. The roof held solidly beneath me as I made my way farther out.

"You finished," I said.

"Yes."

"It's wonderful," I said. And then, "Send up the wine."

He appeared, coming over the side and then settling to sit beside me, sliding the bottle into my lap.

We were quiet for a couple of minutes, each taking our first sip as we surveyed our kingdom, such as it is.

"You did it," I said. "You fixed an unfixable house."

"You helped a smidge."

Why I was so excited over this one small victory, I can't say. I think for both of us, it's just having something complete.

I kept trying to think of what the moon reminded me of, and then I realized it: the zeppelin in my dream. Only because it was equally bright, but it felt like its polar opposite. What I'm trying to say is, it felt like the moon might be a beautiful thing sent from God to make up for zeppelins.

We sipped our wine in silence, perfectly comfortable. I think James and I could never say another word to each other and still be content in each other's presence.

"Do you want to get married, Lenore?" he suddenly asked.

I choked on my wine.

James propped himself on his hands stiffly and laughed. "No, no, not to me. I'm taken, you saucy minx." He shoved my leg with his foot. "I just mean in general. Someday. In the future."

I couldn't answer for a long time. "I don't think about it, really. Beth and I always used to talk and tease about marrying film stars. But now I don't know. What about you? Will you and your fiancée have lots of babies?"

He picked at his trousers, got those shifty eyes again. "I don't know. I want us to be free to do what we want and go where we want."

I ran my hands along the branches.

"I never said thank you," I said. It seemed the right moment.

"For the roof? You can say it now."

I shook my head. "No. For the war. For being in it."

He looked off at nothing. "Don't thank me."

I took another sip of wine.

"Okay. Well then, thank you for the roof," I finally said.

"Thank *you* for letting me share your house."

"Well," I said, "if you really want to thank me, you can go with me to the Fair of Lights. I don't know the city very well, and I can't stand anyone else. Come on an adventure with me.

Let's go be young somewhere for a while. In case you haven't noticed, we're young."

He studied me, making a face that was exaggeratedly exhausted. "But my aching back," he said.

So it's official. I'm going to see the great wonders modern man has to offer with my friend who thinks there's nothing wondrous about man's achievements at all.

And I haven't told you the biggest thing, Beth. I've purposely been sly and saved it to the very end, without any warning whatsoever. So here it is.

I've reached an important milestone in my savings. I reached it three days ago.

Yesterday morning, after my late night on the roof, I got up early and went downtown on a special outing. I walked into the ticket office. And I bought my ticket to America.

After a five-day sail, I'll arrive in New York in two weeks exactly, on June 20.

And I'll make my way to you from there.

I'm sure I'll write you again before I come.

This is really going to happen, Beth.

Love, Lenore

JUNE 7, 1919

Dear Beth,

I'm not sure if I'll send this letter or not.

I woke up last night thinking the room was shaking, but it

was me. Once, before we met—I must have been five or six—I got food poisoning from bad fish, and before I knew I was going to vomit, I thought it was just that I was going to shake apart into a million pieces. That's what it felt like last night. It seemed to me that I couldn't go on being anywhere, in my bed or my room or anywhere else. So I got up and, in my pajamas, I hurried down the stairs and outside, and because it still felt that way—like I couldn't be in the yard either—I kept going, into the woods and all the way to the cottage, and pounded on the door, and when James pulled it open, confused from sleep and blinking at me, I made him open his arms so I could push into them.

He seemed to know what to do, and without any questions he wrapped his arms around me tight, and leaned against the wall.

"I can't breathe," I rasped. I could feel his bare, scarred chest against my cheek, feel the way his skin matted up in thick wrinkles and lines. "I miss him so much it's impossible to go on being a person."

"I know, Allstock."

And then I just cried on him for what seemed forever, and he patted my back saying, "Shh," which is all I really wanted to hear, even though it's meaningless.

I can't stand it when people try to tell me there's some meaning to Teddy dying: that God wanted him in heaven or that he died for the greater good or whatever else. I think maybe "shh" is the only thing you can say for sure without lying.

"Lenore, I don't know anything about anything," James

whispered. "But the important things don't leave us." That I was less sure of. But I didn't protest.

Before dawn I was wiping my face and getting myself together and walking home. James came with me to the edge of the pasture, out of the woods, and then I waded home through the tall grass on my own.

Beth, I've made a discovery, and it's that grief isn't like sadness at all. Sadness is only something that's a part of you. Grief *becomes* you; it wraps you up and changes you and makes everything—every little thing—different than it was before. I remember the me before we got the telegram saying he was gone, but it's like I'm remembering someone else. It feels like an earthquake has gone through me, and the earthquake is that Teddy is gone. And I'm only just beginning to realize it.

And it makes me think about you and me. And how I've wanted so badly to be the person you remember. And how I've hated everyone for their sadness because mine is so big and ugly and hungry inside me that I can't let it catch me.

I've been up all night. I'm lost but I also want to tell you, I'm not hopeless. I can hear the birds waking up, and a line of pretty yellow light is falling into the room, and I feel alive like I haven't in a long time, but also aching. It feels a little like waking up from a fever. Like I've been asleep for months, or a year.

But I can't promise you that I'm unaltered. And I'm not sure anymore that I want to be.

Love, Lenore

JUNE 14, 1919

Beth,

I have so much to tell you that I don't know where to start. Everything has changed. Or more specifically, everything has disappeared.

I keep thinking, should I tell you about the fair? About everything that was wonderful about the night? Or should I skip right to the end, to the parts that really matter?

I suppose it's always best to start things at the beginning, isn't it?

The night of the fair, James showed up at the door at a quarter to seven.

I wore a new turquoise silk dress from Mother, and I knew I looked quite nice (you know I'm not humble). I opened the door and sucked in my breath, because James was in a gray suit and tie, and looked actually nice himself, though I wouldn't have been able to see it before, even if he'd been dressed like that when I first met him.

Mother certainly couldn't. She came up behind me asking about our plans when she brought herself up short at the sight of him, then recovered herself.

"Nice to meet you, James," she boomed with an artificial smile, heartbreaking pity in her eyes, then led us into the drawing room. Father's eyes widened but otherwise he stayed composed, stood from his chair, and shook James's hand.

"Well usually I'd say we've heard nice things about you, but we've heard nothing about you, nice, bad, or otherwise," he said, then cast me a look. "Where did you two meet?"

"We met each other in town," I lied quickly, having rehearsed. "James was looking for fossils. I helped him a little."

Father looked at me suspiciously. "Lenore helps you find rocks?"

"I talked her into it," James said confidently. If he was self-conscious at all, he didn't show it.

We all sat down to chat for a few minutes, and it was strangely like a breath of air in the house, because James was making jokes and giving little compliments about the house, and Father was talking about jobs. And everyone looked happy and relieved—as if I'd finally come to my senses.

"It's nice to have a soldier in the house," Father said. "The others were too young to serve, but you know we lost our own son to the cause."

"I do know, sir."

By the time we set off, Father was patting James on the back as if he were his newfound son-in-law. It was a harmless hope, and I didn't try to signal him otherwise.

We reached the train station with our hearts in our throats—in the crowd, even James seemed to have caught the excitement of where we were headed. The train rocked toward London agonizingly slowly, and the closer we got, the more crowded it became, until it was jammed full of people: laughing teenagers like us, parents and children, old ladies who weren't going to miss their chance to see the sights.

Whenever the train lurched forward, James and I reached to steady each other and laughed.

Getting off at the station, the fair gleamed up ahead of us like a beacon. Even with the throngs of people streaming in around us and through the gates, people were too wrapped up to barely glance at James, and he seemed so at ease it was easy to forget it was crowds that, for months, he'd been wanting to avoid.

He chatted to me as we walked, pointing things out (he has excellent manners when he decides to use them). He even seemed to forget about his face—no touching his lips and his ears or scratching at his cheeks. And I was proud of him, proud to have a hero by my side.

We'd stopped at a booth to gaze at the rows of candy apples, and James had just dug in his pockets to buy us one, when a woman pushed in behind us and said, breathlessly, that they were about to turn on the Hall of Lights. Everyone broke apart as we hurried toward the main plaza, hoping we wouldn't be too late. We weren't. We got there in time to see the lights go on—what they call the great illumination.

I don't care what James says about the industrial age and how it's hurt us just as much as it's helped us. At that moment, when the plaza went up like a flame all around us (so bright that I kept thinking the moon could probably see *us* just as well as we could see *it*), I felt sure that everything that's been invented is all completely perfect, and that human beings are incredible to dream up such things and bring them into being. Aren't we a little like tiny gods? To reach up from the ground for the sun, and then when we can't reach it, to make it ourselves?

We strolled up and down the promenade afterward, in and out of booths. We ate until we felt like we would explode. We rode a Ferris wheel (have you ever been on one?) until I wanted to vomit. And then, it was time to go home. My curfew was one, so we had to leave before the midnight finale.

We dragged our feet all the way back to the station, then caught the first train out feeling both giddy and dejected at the same time. The cars were almost empty, and we were feeling sorry for ourselves despite the fantastic evening, when suddenly there was a ruckus at the back of the car, people pointing and *whooping*. We followed their gazes out the windows to the sky above London, where bright fireworks had just begun to unfurl themselves. We had one of the best views in the house.

"They're to commemorate the fallen," someone said, and everyone took off their hats.

LATER—

I just took a break, but I'm back. I'll get to it now, the part that I don't want to write.

The trains were so much faster coming than going that James and I got back to Forest Row with plenty of time to spare. It was a beautiful night and we were both wide awake, so I decided I'd walk him home along my way.

We stomped into the woods laughing and talking about everything we'd seen. It was a bright night even under the trees, and we barely had to watch where we were going.

Once we got to the cottage, James told me to wait for a second while he ran behind the house to get the lamp for me to take (I knew I didn't need it, but he insisted). I sat inside the room waiting for him, on the edge of his bedroll on the floor. He must have had a hard time finding the lamp, because I waited for a long while, and finally I noticed his rucksack was slightly open, and that a small frame was poking its way out the top. The photo of his fiancée.

I pulled it out to get another look at her. She was just as pretty as I remembered from seeing it the first time—dark-black hair, dark-brown eyes. The inscription on the bottom said: *For my one and only James.*

As I reached to stuff it back into his bag, my hands brushed something wispy and soft, and since I couldn't imagine what it might be, I opened the bag a little wider to see. It was a feather—bundled together with several other treasured things—leaves and such—and bound to some folded papers by a piece of string. I knew I should put it all away, but I thought maybe I could discover who his real family might be. My heart spiked, and I slid the papers out of the string and opened them, glancing quickly at the door. I could still hear James tromping around on the dead leaves behind the cottage.

The bottom page was a wrinkled discharge paper from the hospital six months before, describing his injuries and where they were sustained, which didn't make sense: by a fallen bomb at Warrington Crescent in London.

The second paper was a correspondence from the Department of War, dated a few months before that, a warning that if he did not arrive at the conscription office within the week, it would be considered desertion and prosecuted as such.

And then, on top, was a third piece of paper—a letter.

James,

I apologize for not responding to any of your letters. You'll have heard the news by now that I was married on December 10. I am very happy. It would be inappropriate for us to continue corresponding. Please respect my wishes.

Love, Marie

I was sitting there with the letters spread open in my hands when James finally walked in, but I didn't rush to hide them. He stood still in the doorway when he saw me.

"You weren't in the war?" I said.

He seemed to droop a little, leaning into the doorway. "No."

I took a breath, my thoughts moving fast. "You're hiding here because you don't want to go to jail?"

"Yes."

"You're a coward, then?"

He opened his mouth to say something and then stopped and didn't say anything.

"Teddy's dead," I said flatly, "because he did the right thing.

And you're not, because you didn't." I was squeezing the letter so hard it was slowly ripping apart.

He hung his chin to his chest. "I was afraid," he said.

His words didn't register then, and if they had it wouldn't have mattered. I could only feel the blood rushing in my ears.

"I want you out," I said. "Obviously."

He stood silently for a while, then said simply, "Okay."

"By morning." I laid the letter down at my feet and stood and brushed by him, taking the lamp from his hands.

"Of course."

I'd gone cold and calm inside. I didn't look at him, and I didn't hurry. I just moved out the door and set my feet toward home.

I walked in such a straight line, without moving so much as a branch out of the way, that I was covered in cuts and scratches by the time I got to the house.

I ran the hottest bath possible and now here I am, with this letter to you and a book behind it and a pen balanced on my knees and the hot water stinging all the cuts.

And I keep thinking, of all things—as if it matters—why would James keep all those feathers and leaves with everything else?

The bath has gone cold now, and I have one more thing to write before I head upstairs. Really, it's more of a question.

I knew a boy once, an otherwise smart person, who believed dragons were real until he mentioned it to a teacher and she laughed at him, and he realized how foolish he'd been. It's like me and the Cave of the Cup. All these years, I half believed you'd really found the Grail like you said, even when I was poking fun at it. And now I know how silly that was. And I guess my question is, why did you lie to me, Beth? Why, so many times back then, did you like to tell me my faults? Why did you always tell me I was being bossy when I thought I was being strong? I wonder, are you the person I remember? Were you ever?

It doesn't matter. I'm getting out now to finish packing the last of my things. Bright and early I'll be on my way to the station and dropping this in the post. I'll leave from Southampton tomorrow morning.

I don't know if you'll get this letter before I arrive. I don't know if you'll be waiting for me or not when I catch the train out west. I have so many questions. The biggest one is, will you be happy to see me?

Love, Lenore

ADRI

PART 2

CHAPTER 4

The bright-orange lid of the sun was just rising over the flat horizon. Bleary eyed, Adri flipped back over the pages of the journal and thumbed through Lenore's letters. There had to be an ending somewhere she'd missed. The journal cut off so suddenly. And Lenore's letters were incomplete. Where were the letters that had upset Catherine so much? What had they said?

"You've got to be kidding," she whispered.

She stood, her back aching from sitting for so long. She went and washed her face in the bathroom and then came back, angry and restless. If she'd known she wouldn't be able to finish, she wouldn't have started reading in the first place. It was like spending hours on one of those old jigsaw puzzles with the lighthouses or the majestic herd of horses and then finding out the last pieces were missing. Had Lenore made it to Beth? Had Beezie survived? How had the Ortizes ended up with the farm, when they weren't in the picture at all? Even Galapagos had failed to make an appearance.

Adri rummaged in her nightstand for the postcard she'd found that first night in Canaan, and reread it. After a few moments of going back and forth she realized something wasn't right there either. The postcard was dated May 7, 1920, almost a year after Lenore's last letter. How could Lenore have come to America for the first time twice?

She sank back down into the piles of paper on the bed, burrowing into her pillow, wishing she hadn't stayed up all night for something so pointless. She remembered one of the major reasons she'd always loved her regimen: her runs, her studying, her exhaustive schedule. *This is what happens when you have too much time on your hands. You waste your energy on things that don't matter.*

A sudden sound downstairs jolted her eyes open. A loud, raucous laugh. Had she imagined it?

She followed the smell of coffee to the kitchen where, lounged around the table, were Lily and four other women. They were huddled over handfuls of playing cards, and they looked up as she entered.

"Well if it isn't Rumplestiltskin," a woman said. She and Lily were drinking coffee at the table.

"It's the celebrity," one woman said drolly. And then, standing, "Would you like a beergarita?"

"It's eight in the morning," Adri said, after a moment's confusion.

"Exactly," the woman said, pouring her a glass. "I'm Carol." She and the other women were much younger than Lily—maybe in their seventies. They were all dressed in bright colors, and one wore an orange cloth visor.

"We tried not to wake you," Lily said more kindly.

"I'm the dealer," the woman in the visor said. "Abigail."

"Where'd you all come from?"

"Didn't you know I had friends, honey?" Lily teased. Apparently, Lily wasn't as lonely as she'd thought. Adri felt a stab of jealousy, but she wasn't sure of what—of Lily having four more friends than she did, or of the friends having Lily.

"You said all the people you knew were dead," Adri said, knowing she sounded ridiculous. Lily looked amused.

"Well, that's true, but I made more friends."

"Play a round?" Carol asked.

Adri sank into an empty chair as Carol dealt her a hand ("I used to deal, but I'm too forgetful to do it anymore," Lily said) and before she knew what hit her she was knee-deep in a game of seven-toed Pete.

"You were up late last night." Lily eyed her with concern. "I got up to go to the bathroom around three, and your light was on."

Adri chewed on a thumbnail, still trying to adjust. She felt like she'd spent the night somewhere far away. "Lily, did your mom ever mention any of the Godspeeds by name?"

Lily looked thoughtful for a moment then shook her head.

"Nothing about Catherine, or her sister, Beezie? Or what may have happened to them?"

Lily was about to reply, but Carol cut her off. "Ooh." Carol's eyes widened and she leaned forward. "Yes. The two dead sisters. My friend used to say that if you stood in the yard at midnight, you could hear them coughing." Adri's arms prickled.

"Oh, what a load of bull," Lily said. "I grew up here, and I never heard that. Don't listen to her, Adri, that's just a mean old story."

"Well." Carol gave Lily a firm look. "They died, like, a hundred million years ago. Either way, Lily, it's not like we're hurting their feelings."

"Do you know how they died?" Adri pressed warily.

"Oh, they died of dust pneumonia, very young," Carol said and sorted her cards. "Both of them. Very tragic. It's one of those local stories everyone knows."

Adri's throat hurt began to hurt. "Even the older one?"

"Well, I never heard that." Lily said, squeezing her hands, then seemed to remember herself and pulled her fingers away. "And I live here."

"You heard it, and you don't remember," said Carol.

Lily blew a dubious breath through her lips. "I bet they survived. I bet things worked out for them."

"I think I found those letters your mom had," Adri said.

Lily nodded. "Ooh, I'd love to see them, honey." She looked interested, but not as much as Adri had expected. The women went on with their cards.

"Catherine and Beezie went to this place called the Ragbag Fair," Adri offered, her voice faltering. She felt like everyone had already moved on. "To see a show called the Electric. They got tricked into thinking they could live forever." She stared down at the table and rubbed her thumb against a crack in the wood. She felt heavy and dark.

"The Ragbag Fair," Lily echoed. She looked up. For a moment, her eyes brightened in recognition, then clouded over again. "I knew about that once. You know . . ." And then she tapped her head and rolled her eyes apologetically.

Every weekday, Adri borrowed Lily's car and drove into Wichita for simulations and training. There were zero gravity sessions that made her vomit, launch and landing run-throughs for troubleshooting the dangers of a Mars landing, and engineering sessions where they all took various sections and circuits of the ship apart and put them back together again. Evaluators stood by, studying how each trainee fared, marking things up on a tablet. Adri was always aware of their presence and always keenly aware that they held her future in the balance.

Luckily, she excelled at everything she did. She got to know the belly of her ship the way she'd known the belly of her car. While the others in her group talked between lessons, shared their histories with each other, and started making inside jokes, she focused on redoing things she had already done right, just to make sure.

Whenever one of the other trainees tried to strike up a conversation with her, she answered them in monosyllables.

When Alexa approached her and asked if she wanted a mint (she'd been handing them out), Adri told her without a trace of humor she was trying to quit. And when D'Angelo laid a tray down next to hers at lunch one afternoon and tried to ask her more about herself than just where she was from, she said she had to pee and left. She was never rude exactly, and they all had to interact fairly regularly. She was cooperative and respectful. But she sidestepped any attempts they made to get to know her.

In the evenings, Adri searched the house for more evidence of the Godspeeds' fate, or of Lenore's arrival in Canaan. She connected Lily's Curiosity chip to her ear and searched online, breaking a rule only to turn up nothing but that the Allstocks had been a wealthy family who'd made their fortune during the industrial revolution and a picture of Lenore (a dark beauty in a nice dress, fuzzy and unfocused).

In the house, there was plenty of evidence of their lives. She now knew that the dusty copies of *Grimm's Fairy Tales* and *Ethan Frome* had been Lenore's and then Beth's. But there was no sign of how things had ended for them. And Adri was so methodical, so thorough, she knew that if anything had been left behind, a few hours would have been enough to find it.

She tried to shake the dead people out of her mind, but she

couldn't shake the mystery of them. She couldn't help seeing them layered on the landscape around her—in the decaying bunkhouse, in the view of the abandoned farm that had once belonged to the Chiltons.

Finally one morning, Lily—seeing her thumbing through the bookshelves for more letters that might have fallen between the volumes—shuffled up behind her. "You're like a dog with a bone," she said.

Adri looked up at her. "I just hate loose ends. They annoy me." There was more to it than that, but it embarrassed her to say so. And she didn't understand herself why it mattered.

"You should try the library," Lily said. "They have some local records that probably wouldn't make it online."

"This podunk town has a library?" Adri asked, disbelieving.

"Yeah, the Podunk Regional Library," Lily offered blandly. "Off Main Street."

The following morning, a Saturday, she followed Lily's directions. She found her way to the library on her run, her breath puffing out behind her in the cold. It was down a street off Main that said *No Outlet*, its windows brightly lit in the gray morning air. She slowed and walked back and forth past the front door a few times, hands on her hips to catch her breath, and then walked inside.

Most libraries were sleek and bookless information hubs, good places to search for archived content that wasn't online. The Huygens Library on Mars looked out of enormous windows onto a canyon, and there you could print 3D replicas of almost any landscape or house or cell structure you could find online or in the data archives, you could check out soils, or skeletons, or fossils, or Pixos that projected old concerts all around you. This place smelled like paper.

A young man came walking out from behind a desk to the right. "Can I help you with something?"

"I'm looking for information about someone who used to live in town. Catherine Godspeed. Or her mother, Beth."

The man studied her for a second, then smiled. "You're Lily's cousin. The famous one."

Adri blinked at him, surprised.

"You're in the local paper, didn't you know? Do you want to see it?"

"Um . . ." Adri shook her head. "No."

The man looked slightly disappointed. He introduced himself as Steven, pulled out two chairs that stood in front of an archaic-looking machine. "I may be able to help. We have some really old microfiche that were supposed to go online but never did. Clippings from the *Canaan Sentinel*, local stuff. If they're not online, they may be there. Birth announcements and public records and things like that. It's such a small town almost everyone's made it into the paper at some point."

Adri sat down as Steven powered up the old machine. They scrolled back to the years that she wanted and began scanning the headlines.

As promised, there were front page articles about people's blue ribbon pumpkins and a collision between a car and a beloved turkey. Still, most of the headlines were about the Dust Bowl:

Violent Storms Dim Capitol for Five Hours

Mayor Pleads for Government Aid

Roosevelt Blames Farmers for Dust

"Poor people," Steven said, scrolling through one article after another. "All these investors give them incentives to move to 'the breadbasket' and farm the land. But the farmers don't know that the bluestem and buffalo grass they're tearing up is what holds the soil in such a windy place. Then comes a drought, and up goes the dirt."

"They should have known better," Adri said. She leaned her chin on her hand and stared at the headlines: more bad news as the years stretched on.

Dust Reaches Statue of Liberty

Roosevelt Urges Federal Relief

She relaxed into her chair, the warmth of the room making her drowsy. Then a headline blinked onto the screen, and Steven let out a pleased "huh."

November 15, 1935: Government Offers Resettlements

The point of interest was not the headline but the caption, which lay beneath a grainy photograph of a skinny severe-looking woman standing on the front porch of the house where Adri now lived.

Mrs. Beth Godspeed is one of the many local farmers who've sold part of her land for government resettlement, following the deaths of her husband and daughters.

Adri sat for a few minutes in silence, feeling Steven's eyes on her. So it was true, they had both died the year that Catherine had written in her journal, though it didn't make any sense. Catherine had never been sick. Her heart sank.

"Would you be able to find out where they're buried?" she asked.

"There's nothing," Steven said after ten more minutes of searching. "A lot of the cemeteries were private back then . . . family plots, stuff like that—nothing official." He thought for a second. "You could put in a request at the archives in Wichita. They carry records on so many of those families—death certificates, things like that. If you wanted a death record."

Adri didn't think she wanted a death record.

She thanked Steven and, her chest aching, walked out into the cold, zipping her fleece over her chin.

All the way home she practiced the positive visualization techniques she'd learned in school growing up. She tried to visualize herself on Mars, doing her work, looking down on the landscape from her apartment in the dome. She wanted to be practical.

She couldn't explain how her heart felt like rocks in her feet, weighing her down. It shouldn't matter whether Catherine and Beezie died in the dust or fifty years later of natural causes. They'd all been dead for so long that even their grandchildren were dead.

Why should she grieve for people she never even knew?

CHAPTER 5

The sky was slate gray for the first half of November. Adri's trips to Wichita began to feel routine, and she got more and more nervous about her one-on-one meeting with Lamont. She wanted the certainty of him signing his name to the contract and her signing her own.

In those weeks, Kansas was more bone-chillingly cold and wind-whipped than she could have imagined, but she tried to appreciate it while it lasted. There would be no seasons in the Bubble; it was always a perfect seventy-two degrees. At noon every day she started mixing an Optimal Protein shake and took the new supplement that had been prescribed for the forty-five days leading up to launch.

She drove past the Wichita Archives each time she headed in and out of the city, but never stopped.

The day after Thanksgiving (a printed meal of turkey and mashed potatoes, eaten in front of the woodstove) Lily came down the attic ladder, her arms full of little plastic angels. "I forgot I had these! I got them at the Nickel & Dollar. They were so cheap I got twenty," she said. "Santa's coming, and I'm not even ready."

"It's still November," Adri said. Earlier, they'd filled Galapagos's shed with fresh warm hay and turned on an electric heater. Already Lily had put up an anemic Christmas tree in the library and a manger with the baby Jesus, which she adjusted just so in what she called *the place of honor.* "And I read somewhere the other day that Santa's not real," Adri offered.

"I think the Grinch has been spreading that rumor," Lily said and ascended the ladder again.

"You're too old for that," Adri called up to her, looking at Lily's feet. "Your bones are brittle, and you could break something if you fell." Lily ignored her.

Adri was on the parlor couch reading when her cousin finally came downstairs for good, closing up the attic with a creak, her white hair askew and her shirt bunched up on one side under her bra.

"Well, it's no use," she said.

"What, perpetuating lies about the red-suited fat man?"

Lily rolled her eyes. "I wasn't even doing Christmas stuff anymore, smarty. I was just seeing if there were any relics to help us"—she tugged her shirt down and smoothed her hair—"to figure out about the house, about those girls from the letters you found. I guess I don't have anything for you. Looks like you just get coal again this year."

"That's okay. I've never really been on the nice list," Adri said. "And we already know everything there is to know. They died. End of story."

Lily sighed and sank down onto the couch. She shook her head. "I keep thinking there's something I wanted to tell you. About the Ragbag Fair. But each time it comes back to me, it slips out of my head before I can get my words together." She shook her head, frustrated. She gazed around. "Don't you wish you could gaze into the bones of any place? A house or a field or a tree, and see its secrets?"

"Trees don't have bones," Adri said, but Lily went on, ignoring her.

"I could tell every detail of my favorite rain boots when I was four years old. I can see them as if I were wearing them yesterday. But so many other things, I forget. I guess I'm like my grandpa now." Lily was amused and forlorn at the same time. "Permanently confused."

Adri knew she should reach for her hand, to give her an encouraging squeeze. She curled her fingers but didn't move them.

"Well, I know my guardian angels are watching out for me

anyway," Lily said. And then, suddenly brightening, as if this led her to an idea, "Do you want to see where I'm gonna live?" she suddenly asked. "When my brain's finally . . ." Lily pantomimed an explosion with her hands.

The Holy Redeemer Home for the Aged lay on the edge of God's View, one town away. It looked more like a small strip mall than a home. It sprawled over two acres, enclosed by a cement wall.

"So us crazy ones don't wander off," Lily said as they approached the entrance.

Inside, the place was bustling. A room to the right was full of people playing bingo, in another large living room a woman was playing records. There were more people in Holy Redeemer than Adri had seen altogether since she got to Canaan.

"My fellow earth ruiners," Lily said with a wink, as they watched people push their bingo chips around. Two women held hands, white haired and hunched over a table, one reading to the other.

The whole place was a contrast: homey yet not home, cozy yet institutional. It was a nice place, but of course, nothing like Lily's own house.

Lily sighed. "I guess this is *my* Mars," she said. "That I'll be launching off to someday. Someday soon, I guess. Planet of the Old People." She looked around, resigned, accepting. "You think you fade," she said. "You *look* like you fade. But believe me, you don't."

Adri was silent. What could she say to that?

• • •

On the ride home, she tried to be upbeat, to agree with Lily that it was "such a lovely place," but she kept sinking into silence. Finally, she forced herself to say what was on her mind.

"Hey, Lily? If you knew about me for so long, why didn't you ever call me? Or write me? Or tell me you were here? How come you never wanted to know me?"

Lily looked over at her, surprised. "Well, I wrote them about it. I called. For a while after . . . the flood, your parents . . . I thought maybe I could adopt you. But they said I was past the age limit. And that it would be disruptive; you were doing so well in school. And I thought, well, maybe you just didn't have any use for some old fart in Nowhere, Kansas. Maybe I assumed that you just wouldn't think much of me."

Adri stared out the window.

"Was that wrong? Have I hurt you?" Lily asked, her eyes big and uncertain.

Adri swallowed. "No."

"It always made me happy to know you were there, doing well," Lily went on. "I always felt like you were partly mine. Like, part of my life."

Adri nodded. "Thanks, Lily."

Would it have changed anything if she'd known? Would she have turned out to be better—just better in general at all the things she was bad at with people—if she'd had someone in her life like Lily? Would she have been better at touching someone on the hand to console them? Would she be going to Mars at all?

The city fell away quickly, and they entered the open plains, the vast expanses of land people had left behind over the years of drought and never come back to. Then Lily did something unexpected. She rolled down the window and pressed her face to the frigid air. She breathed deeply.

"Life is sweet, isn't it?" she said.

CHAPTER 6

The ride to Wichita on December 7 was glitteringly cold and bright. Lily, bored, had wanted to come along. She separated from Adri at the Center's waiting room, but not before telling her she looked like death.

"Lighten up. They love you," she said. "He'll sign the contract. Geez, you worry too much."

Adri rolled her eyes and then went to the front desk to check in.

Lamont met her at the double doors of the secured-access section and led her back, a large coffee in one hand. His office was spacious but decidedly not edgy for someone with so much power. Photos of his family flickered across one wall and there was a nice view of downtown, but otherwise it was a simple, mostly empty space. He gestured to a chair across from him as he sat down and took a sip of his coffee.

"Don't be nervous, Adri. This meeting is a good thing for both of us. Okay?"

Adri nodded. He pulled a folder toward him, opened it, and looked over the first page. "Your specialty is life systems. You've never had a grade lower than an A. You're a stellar athlete. You're staying with your cousin, Lily, nearby. No other family, yes?"

Adri nodded.

Lamont sank back in his chair. "I remember reading your application. I fought for you."

"Fought for me?"

"Well, the board was concerned. As you know, we generally like to recruit people who play well with others. Your records indicate you're a bit of a loner. You're the only recruit who hasn't complained that disabling your devices has made it hard for you to communicate with friends and loved ones."

"For me, your work ethic, your big brain, and your character won the day." He closed the notebook. "And it still does. We're not thrilled that you haven't connected with the other recruits. The bonds you're able to form with your teammates matter to us. But you're respectful, you cooperate, you're very disciplined. So as far as I'm concerned, we're happy with you. Ready to sign you."

Adri stared at the closed book, relieved and confused at the same time.

"That's it?" she said.

"Well, not quite."

"Not quite?"

"Well, it's a two-way street. Are you happy with us? Do you still want to go?"

"Yes."

Lamont studied her. Apparently, it wasn't so simple as saying yes.

"Adri, it's our business to know you a little better than you know yourself, in some ways. Our psychologists know this kind of stuff backward and forward. And to me . . . to us . . . you seem to be holding back."

"Holding back how?" Adri asked, swallowing, disbelieving.

"I see most recruits come through here, they're scared, they're nervous, but they're *engaged.* They want to get to know the people they're going to be living with, potentially for the rest of their lives. Adri, I said it's fine with me if you keep to yourself generally, but I wonder, is it fine with *you*? Are you truly *excited* about all of this? Are you ready to live and work with all these folks? Because you'll need their support in the challenging times ahead, just as they'll need yours."

Adri searched for something to say but came up blank. "I can't be who I'm not," she finally said. She didn't add that she had wanted to, and tried, and given up.

"Look," Lamont went on. "I'm not trying to give you a hard

time. But it costs us forty million dollars per person to send you to space. We don't plan on ever bringing you back. So I want to know you're in a good place . . ."

"I'm in a good place."

"Because you don't have to go. You really don't."

It was the first time the thought of not going . . . of her own free will . . . had occurred to her, even as a remote possibility. She thought what the future would look like if she could settle back into what she knew, back into life on Earth. What if she did stay with Lily, made a life in a dead town? It was seductive—the lack of fear that went with that possibility. Even the comfort of knowing Lily would have her. It sounded so easy.

"Tell you what," Lamont said after studying her. "I'm not going to have you sign a contract today. As far as I'm concerned, you're in. But if you want to back out, at any time before the launch, you come to me, okay?"

"I'm not backing out," Adri said. "It's not going to happen."

"In the meantime," Lamont went on, ignoring her, "whatever you need to wrap up to get closure on your life here, I recommend you do it. You need to call your long-lost friend and apologize for something, you do it. If it's costly, like say, you really want to make Lily's dreams of seeing the Taj Mahal a reality or whatever, you let me know. That's no problem for us. You have great value to this mission, and we can do almost anything if it helps you firm up your commitment."

"There's nothing," Adri said. "I don't need anything."

"Okay," Lamont said, but he shuffled his papers and put them away. “We envision the next four weeks as ‘wrapping up’ time. Stay healthy, keep up with your Biphosphonates, wash and sanitize your hands constantly. Even a cold could jeopardize your spot on this particular launch.

“And I’m serious about the closure. The next four weeks are going to go faster than you can imagine. Get your affairs in order. Be good to yourself.”

Lily was on her second cup of hot chocolate when Adri found her in the lounge. “A robot named Jeeves gave it to me,” she said, delighted. “I love it here.” They got into the car.

“How’d it go?”

Adri looked at her. “He says to start wrapping things up.” She didn’t want to go into the rest.

“Like what?”

Adri thought for a long time. “Do you mind if we go to the archives?” Adri said.

“Why?”

“Apparently, people need closure,” she said. “It’s some kind of a thing.”

The Wichita Historical Archives were housed in an enormous, carved marble building that looked out on the river, brand new and elegant and beautiful. Its many quiet, cavernous rooms were divided into two sections: records and exhibits. The exhibits—full of life-size photos, historical artifacts, dioramas—specialized in portions of Kansas’s history, such as the Breadbasket boom, migrant workers, the recession and reboot of the 2020s, the shifting of the space program to Wichita. It didn't take long to find the exhibit on the Dust Bowl.

Adri and Lily trailed through the room slowly, gazing at the enormous sepia-toned photos of prairie land covered in jackrabbits, herds of skeletal cattle, breathtaking shots of dust clouds dwarfing the tiny towns they were swooping in to envelop. It was eerie—after reading about it in Catherine's words—to see it so starkly depicted, like a dark fairy tale coming to life. The whole thing was so scary, so beautiful, that it could easily have been make-believe.

"That's only three decades before I was born," Lily said, pointing to a photo of a ramshackle old hut, a stoic, embattled family standing on its porch, with *June 1935* engraved along the bottom. "They should put *me* in this museum."

"I saw a tiger once," Adri replied. "At this traveling science exhibit in Miami. Even then, they seemed otherworldly. Like, how could they exist? Doesn't it seem like . . . how could something so powerful and strange exist?"

Tigers didn't live in the wild now. It seemed like nobody did. She wasn't being logical, but Lily nodded.

"Isn't it funny?" Lily finally said.

"What?"

"Well, you don't like anybody. But you care so much about what happened to these people you've never met, that you read about in a pile of papers."

"I'm just frustrated. I like to finish things."

But Lily pushed on. “Why do you think that is, that you love these people you don’t know?”

Adri shook her head. “I don’t. I’m just curious.”

Lily shrugged. Offhandedly, as they were leaving the room, she said, “Maybe it’s because you’re invisible to them. Maybe that’s why you let them in.” She tapped on the wall on her way out, as if for good luck. “It’s less scary that way.”

“Ugh,” Adri said. “Did anyone ever tell you you’re not, like, an ancient oracle, you just look like one?”

Lily laughed at that.

They made their way down a long hallway to the opposite side of the building, where the records were housed. Adri filled out a long form that specified what she was after:

Your address: 268 Jericho Road, Canaan, KS 67124
Searching for records related to which person(s):
Catherine Godspeed, Beezie Godspeed, Beth Abbott Godspeed
Timeframe: 1934–1940
Last known locality of person(s): Canaan, Kansas

When she brought the paper up to the man behind the front desk, he glanced over it quickly, then smiled.

“All righty. We’ll let you know.”

“You mean I don’t get to see anything today?” Adri was disbelieving, crestfallen.

He shook his head. "Some of the records are housed off-site because there's just not enough room. We'll be in touch if we have any success. If you haven't heard from us in six weeks or so, it means nothing came up related to your criteria. But we'll send you a slip in the mail to confirm."

"Six weeks?" She'd be long gone by then. "It's not like I'm asking for you guys to find Amelia Earhart's bones, I'm just looking for some records that already belong to this archive." Lily shot her a look, so she added, "Sir."

The man was unmoved.

"I'm sorry about my cousin," Lily said. "She doesn't have parents. She's from Florida. She was raised by dolphins."

Back in the car, Lily looked around, a little disoriented. "Why did we just go there?" she asked.

Adri turned to her, confused. "We were looking for the Godspeeds, remember?"

"Oh, right," Lily said. But it was clear she was just pretending to remember.

CHAPTER 7

Christmas Eve, Adri found Lily stringing popcorn at the kitchen table, snow falling past the window behind her, looking forlorn. She stood in the doorway, watching her. She tried to picture how different life would look if she stayed—how this might be the next five Christmases, or ten.

"Hey, you wanna hang out tonight?" she asked. It wasn't that she felt sorry for her, but that she liked Lily and wanted the company.

Lily looked up, surprised, and beamed. "I'd love it."

They watched old movies. Adri fed the woodstove, and they both curled under the same big blanket.

"It's a slumber party," Lily declared, walking back and forth to get a soda, or a bowl of ice cream. She was too excited to sit still.

She made Adri open three Christmas presents early: two were little ceramics she'd painted at a craft class with Carol, and one was just a bundle of Christmas lights.

"You bought me Christmas lights for Christmas," Adri said. She hadn't gotten anything for Lily in return.

Lily looked at the lights for a moment and then held her hands out, palms up. "Well, it's just nice to have something to unwrap, isn't it?" She took the lights out of Adri's hands and began to string them along the branches of the tree.

"I don't know. So much plastic. Stuff like that is a waste." She couldn't stop herself.

"You should just say thank you, dummy."

"You should be less wasteful," Adri said dryly. But there was a knot in her throat, and they both sat in silence for a while.

"Adri, I love you even when you're judging me," Lily said and popped some more popcorn in her mouth.

Adri looked out the window, toward the shed. The word made her uncomfortable, and she didn't know how Lily felt like she knew her enough to love her.

"I have an awkward question," she finally said. Lily cocked her head inquisitively, then nibbled a kernel from where she'd placed it on her shoulder as a joke.

"What will really happen to Galapagos?"

"She'll be fine here with me."

"But . . . when you're . . . not here anymore."

"Yeah, yeah, I get it. I don't know. I guess whoever took her from the wild should never have taken her in the first place, when you think about it in the long term."

"Do you think she could ever go back to the wild?"

Lily gazed out the window, her eyebrows descending. "She's a tough old thing. I'd take her somewhere and set her free if I had the courage . . . a wild animal should be wild. But she's been in captivity almost her whole life."

They both stared out the window at the tortoise, who'd poked her head out of the shed to gaze over the pasture.

"I think she'd make it, though." Lily sighed. "She'll outlive us all, just watch."

"Lily? Do you think you'll remember me? Like, as your dementia gets worse?"

Lily blinked at her. Her mouth turned down at the corners. "I don't know. I wish I could promise you that I'll remember you to the day I die. But I can't. This getting old is the pits, Adri. I'm glad you don't have to worry about it for a long, long time."

Adri nodded. "Yeah."

"Don't fall asleep," Lily finally said. "I don't want this to end. If you fall asleep before me, I'll write something on your forehead. *Fart.* Something like that."

But after another twenty minutes it was Lily who was nodding off. At one point she startled awake, yawned and stretched, and said, "It's a great feeling, isn't it? When someone in the house stays awake after you?" And then she fell right back asleep.

Adri gazed around the room, at all the old books that had belonged to Lenore, to Beth, then to Catherine. She felt more lonely than she could ever remember feeling, and she didn't know why. She was thinking about libraries, used gum, bus stops, red lights, convenience stores. All these things she'd never noticed, stupid things, even things she didn't like. How she'd taken these things for granted, and she was never going to see them again. Dancers glided across the TV screen to old-fashioned music.

"Lily?" she whispered. Lily didn't move. "Can I tell you something?" Lily breathed deeply, clearly asleep. "I think all my life my heart's been broken," Adri whispered, "and I didn't even notice. And I don't even know by what."

It wasn't because of any one thing—not losing parents she didn't remember, not growing up in the group home—not the obvious things. It felt more like it had just come from being born, from time existing.

Lily pulled the blanket tighter up under her own chin, the lights of the TV flickering across her face, and snored.

CHAPTER 8

If Lily knew Adri's birthday was December 27, she'd forgotten, which was the way Adri preferred it. The day came and went without fanfare, and on January 30, she and three other Colonists—Saba, D'Angelo, and Alexa—set off for the East Coast portion of the Expeditions publicity tour.

The first stop was New York, where they were scheduled for three morning shows and then an afternoon packed with functions around the city. A stylist dressed and made them up that morning, working her way through Adri's tangled, unbrushed hair, and their publicist coached them in the car. Compared to her usual sloppiness Adri's made-up face and hair felt pasted on and strange.

"Convince the taxpayers and shareholders that they're making a good investment. Convince them you're earning your keep. Adri, practice smiling."

They sipped coffee with the hosts and repeated the same talking points: that Mars was full of mineral exports to justify its costliness, that it had four seasons like Earth and 664 days a year. Adri and Saba offered technical information, while D'Angelo and Alexa won people over with their charm.

Adri had only ever seen Manhattan on TV. That evening, she gazed from their shared hotel suite in Midtown toward the old part of the city, the empty skyscrapers of the financial district glinting at sunset. That part of the island was dark, waterlogged, impassable—not viable as a place to live anymore, river water obscuring the streets. Giant electronic banners stood at the top of some of the abandoned towers. *Use Ivory Soap*! one said.

The others stayed up late to play cards, taking puffs of cigars (there'd be no tobacco at all on Mars, so now was their chance), and drinking tiny bottles of vodka that arrived through the bar via glowing pneumatic tubes. Adri went into her room to read a city travel guide. From her room she could hear them learning things about each other: how Saba had weirdly chubby thumbs, how D'Angelo managed to be both a shameless flirt and socially awkward at the same time, that Alexa was a walking pharmacy, always keeping a bag on her full of cough drops and Band-Aids and hand sanitizer and bottled water.

Around 11:30, D'Angelo appeared in her doorway, pushing it open gingerly.

"Adri? Aren't you going to watch the ball drop with us?"

"I don't think so," Adri said.

But instead of leaving, he pushed farther into her room. He had a weird look on his face, mischievous. "I really think you should."

"I'm not really into that stuff," she said.

He leaned down and linked his arm through hers, giving her a big cheesy grin.

"Come on. Everyone insists."

Adri didn't know how to keep saying no without being rude, so she stood up and followed him into the living room, where everyone was gathered around a cake, with eighteen candles lit.

"Is that for me?" Adri asked flatly.

"Sorry it's late," Alexa said. "Lamont only just told us this morning. He sent us a message."

The cake said, in glowing yellow words on chocolate icing, *Happy Birthday, Minty.*

"That's what we call you behind your back," Alexa explained, "since you said you're trying to quit mints."

Adri was painfully embarrassed and flattered at the same time. And guilty. She couldn't understand why they'd taken the time to do it. And she liked that she had a nickname, even if it was making fun of her.

As they ate popcorn and watched TV, Adri was quiet, but not unhappy, her knees up to her chin and her arms folded around them. D'Angelo and Alexa were flirting, and Saba had already established herself as the practical one—reminding them that they had to be up at 4:30 the next morning and that she was going to bed at 12:01. Everyone went out of their way to include Adri, trying to get her to puff a cigar, fixing her a drink.

The night devolved after that, into laughter (even, a few times, hers) and a few strange confessions. Saba admitted that she was terrified of flying, and everyone found that hilarious. D'Angelo admitted he'd started studying for the Expeditions requirements in fifth grade, to try to impress a girl. Adri didn't reveal anything about herself, but she also didn't walk away.

Sitting there, she felt a part of them. And she found that, the more they talked about what was coming, the more she wanted to be. She wanted to go to Mars, as badly as she ever had. In the fear of going, it was sometimes easy to forget it.

As they waited for the moment the ball would drop, the TV showed footage of celebrations that had happened all over the world already: in Sydney, Tokyo, Moscow.

"Next time we watch this," Saba said, "it'll be like—*there they are on that other planet, celebrating New Year's.* It won't be *our* New Year anymore. Doesn't that feel crazy?"

Everyone was quiet for a long time.

"Earth," Alexa finally said. "It's not that great anyway." And they all smiled sadly. Because, of course, it was everything.

Pulling into Canaan in the back of a private car, Adri's heart lifted the closer they got to the farm. She was eager and excited to see Lily, more eager than she would have thought.

Turning into the driveway, she could see Galapagos craning her neck and then launching into her version of a run, which was really a slow walk. By the time she climbed out of the cab, the tortoise had just made it past the edge of the pond toward her. Adri climbed over the leaning fence and knelt next to her, scratching her neck. Galapagos rolled her eyes, luxuriating. "I missed you too, you inscrutable little weirdo. Aren't you cold?"

Lily was in the kitchen, bent under the sink, sniffling and rubbing her sleeve along the bottom of her nose, which was unlike her, her hair messy and unwashed. When Adri said hello she *thwapped* her head against the cabinet, and then leaned back to peer up at her.

"Damn pipe is broken," she said, by way of explanation and hello.

Adri gazed around. There were dishes piled in the sink. It was unbearably hot, and when she looked at the thermostat, the heat had been turned up to ninety-six degrees.

Adri turned it down as Lily came to sit at the table.

"How was your trip?" she asked.

"It was good," Adri said uncertainly.

"Well that's good." Lily gazed around at the kitchen as if she didn't want to meet Adri's eyes.

Adri sat down across from her, picking at the edges of the table, unsure what she was supposed to do.

"Have you been okay here?" she asked.

Lily gazed at her for a few minutes sheepishly, then nodded.

• • •

Adri unpacked and showered quickly so she could make it back down to Lily. But she couldn't find her in the kitchen or the living room.

She went back upstairs to look in her bedroom, didn't find her there, and then, just as she was about to leave, caught a glimpse of her out the window.

Lily was standing next to Galapagos in the pasture, petting the tortoise's head and looking around. She'd brought out a pile of blankets that lay in a lump beside them.

Adri hurried outside and crossed the grass toward her.

"Lily, are you okay?"

"Yeah, I just thought she might be cold," Lily said.

Adri looked down at the blankets, then at Lily. Lily folded her hands together at her waist, studying them, and then glanced up at her.

"I don't remember where I am. Can you help me?" she asked. "Can you call a doctor?"

CHAPTER 9

After they sat in triage for half an hour, a nurse admitted Lily and brought her into a room in the back of the small hospital. Adri excused herself while Lily was changed into a gown and a doctor came in to examine her.

When she entered the room again, Lily was back in her clothes and lying on top of the white sheets under the yellowish glow of the ceiling lights.

"Where's your gown?"

"I hate those things. I changed back."

"But you're not supposed to."

"What are they going to do to me? Put me in jail?"

Adri was tempted to touch her arm as she approached her but instead sat on a chair beside her.

"So what happened?" she asked.

Lily laughed. "I got old, that's what happened."

"My housemate's grandma lived to be a hundred and twenty-two," Adri offered.

"Well la-di-da for her."

"Seriously, can you describe what happened?"

Lily smiled at her. "I *am* serious. I'm old. Things just give out. They can call it dementia or whatever else, but the condition is really just being a human for too long."

"I'm sorry, Lily."

"Don't be sorry. Geez. It's the toll you pay for riding. You know? They've cured a lot of things. Just not my brain. It's like molasses swamp in there."

Adri didn't know. She didn't know, now, if she'd ever have to pay the toll. Her life would stretch on and on. And Lily had missed that boat. And it seemed horribly unfair.

"I've been thinking about it," Lily finally said. "And I wanted to say I'm sorry."

"For what?"

Lily chewed on her bottom lip thoughtfully, frowning at the horrible ceiling tiles above her. "Maybe we did make some big mistakes, us older people. And now you have to pay. Maybe you were right when you said I could have done things better."

"I didn't say . . ."

"I . . . I don't think most of us were trying to ruin anything."

Lily sighed. "The longer I live," she looked up at the ceiling, "the more I think our big mistakes are not about having bad intentions, but just not paying attention. Just bumbling along, a little self-absorbed." Lily looked thoughtful for a moment. "Plus a few major assholes, I guess."

She looked up at Adri. "I'm sorry to say I think you'll make just as many mistakes as I did. Just different mistakes."

"I have to hope for more than that," Adri said.

"Yeah, of course." Lily reached for a cup of water on her bedside table and took a sip, then laid it down, and laid back again.

"You know," she said softly, with a tiny hint of a sad smile. "I envy you. I'm happy for you; I'd give you anything I had if I could, but I envy you." She smiled. "You'll go up into the sky and you'll never come back down, it's like defying one of the oldest laws in the book. But that's the way it goes, I guess. *You* get the future, not me. It's just . . . I wish I could be in your shoes for a minute or two. Feel the future you feel." She reached out and patted Adri's hand. "I'll tell you a secret. I like to say I'm a has-been, but I don't really mean it. I feel young too. I feel like this old body has nothing to do with me at all."

"I thought they couldn't pay you a million dollars to live longer."

Lily shrugged. "I think that's what you say when you can't have something you want, isn't it? You say you don't want it in the first place."

They were silent for a long while.

"I don't know anything about anything, Adri. But I know I

love you. And I don't care if it's because of evolution or whatever else. I feel it anyway. It doesn't matter what it's for."

"Why do you love me?" Adri asked, looking anywhere but Lily's eyes.

Lily looked surprised by the question. She seemed to realize she didn't have the perfect answer because she held up her hands sheepishly, tubes dangling.

"Why not?" she finally said.

She was released two days later. They had dinner then watched a show called *Baked!* where you could watch someone make desserts from the best restaurants around the world, and then for a few dollars print them out yourself if you had the right feedstocks.

That night they had a snowstorm. They watched the flakes swirl across the fields, blindingly bright and white. They watched a sitcom with the storm as a backdrop.

They were halfway through a commercial for Bexie dolls (Adri liked to pop their heads off when she was little but now they were indestructible and could make you chocolate milk and learn all your habits by heart) when Lily said, apropos of nothing, "One more week." She gave a forced, fake smile.

It was what Adri had been thinking all day. Her heart pounded as she tried to voice what she'd been thinking since New York, since even before. The first couple times she tried, she couldn't get it out.

"What if I could bring you with me?" she finally asked. "To Mars?"

Lily's eyes flashed with surprise.

"Lamont said I could ask for anything. What if I asked for that? He might say yes."

Lily stared at her solemnly for a long while, and then smiled. "Who wants to go to Mars?" she teased.

"Seriously."

"Adri, you know they don't do that. Otherwise everyone would be taking their families with them." Lily opened her palms on her lap, stared at her fingers for a moment. "Besides, I wouldn't go. Not even if they let me."

There was so much finality in her voice.

"I could stay with you," she offered, her voice cracking half-way through. A flutter of fear rose up in her chest, and she didn't know whether she was scared most of yes or no.

Lily looked up at her, frowning. A long moment passed, what felt like an eternity, where they teetered there—between one thing and another, each thing a completely different life for both of them. Then finally, Lily spoke.

"Now, that would kill me. It truly would. If you wanted to take away all my happiness, you could do that."

Adri looked down at her hands, embarrassed, relieved, deeply disappointed, still afraid.

"Your happiness is my happiness. Don't you understand that, Adri?"

Adri shook her head. "No."

"I hope one day you do," Lily said.

They watched the snow a while longer. Adri was going. She

would go. This was the moment it was being settled, she realized.

"Pass the time for me," Lily finally said. "Tell me about our girls—the two dead sisters. Tell me about the best friends on either side of the Atlantic. Maybe I'll remember it all better if I hear it from you."

So Adri did. She told her about Catherine and Beezie Godspeed and their irresistible farmhand, Ellis. She told her about Lenore Allstock, whose friend in America was not the friend she thought she was.

And Lily remembered. Adri told the story in such detail that when, two days later, the letter arrived from the Wichita Archives, Lily was as eager to open it as she was.

She raced inside to give it to Adri and stood with her hands clasped tightly as Adri tore the seal. It was a simple, short form letter.

We are sorry, but no records match your criteria.

They stood for a moment.

"Maybe they didn't die," Lily said.

"Yeah," Adri said. "Maybe they're still living in the attic."

Lily got that the joke was on her, but she jumped on the train anyway. "Maybe they're zombies," she said.

CHAPTER 10

The week of launch, Adri drank a special shake four times a day and ate bars laced with electromagnetic proteins in order to have her vitals monitored at all times. She dropped her exercise routine per Lamont's instructions in order to, as the Institute put it, "rest, revive, spend time with your loved ones, and say good-bye."

The launch was Sunday. Wednesday afternoon, Adri began to pack. She piled things onto her bed that would be disastrous to forget. She weighed her belongings on a scale the Center had provided. They were allowed twenty-five pounds for personal items—enough for clothes, a special piece of jewelry maybe or a favorite stuffed animal from childhood, things like that. She was saddened to see—looking at the scale—that she didn't need to weed anything out.

Lily was quiet that afternoon. They played cards and mostly hid from the winter weather, watched TV, ate. They did nothing particularly worthy of a person's last two days on Earth. Time was speeding up, and they couldn't stop it.

Late that night they were watching a newscast about some political debate revolving around the observatories on the moon and who owned which territories. Adri was drifting off when Lily suddenly clutched her arm, her fingers digging in like claws.

"I remember."

Adri tried to comprehend her, half asleep, focusing on the room.

But Lily only dug her fingers in harder. "I remember where the Electric used to be."

Neither of them could stand to wait until morning.

They passed the place three times before they finally stopped; it was so easy to miss in the dark, surrounded by an old metal fence alongside the road. Adri had passed it many times on her runs: an unassuming lot overgrown with weeds and tall grass, with an ancient real estate sign (*Commercially Zoned*) dangling from the mesh of the fence. Climbing out of the car, Adri's pulse sped up.

"They were supposed to build on it, before the 2020

economic reboot," Lily explained, pulling her coat and hood tightly around her as they stepped over the leaning fence. The whole place was desolate, unprotected from the frigid wind. "I remember coming here as a kid, looking for old coins with a metal detector. We all used to do that. Somebody found a box full of silver dollars once."

Lily walked deeper and deeper into the tall grass ahead of her. "Well, where do we start?" she asked. They gazed at each other, shivering, and then Lily looked at the ground around her feet and started beating back the tall grass. After twenty minutes they'd turned up three old Coke cans and a pair of bike tires.

"We'll never find anything," Adri said, knowing they were being ridiculous, because what were they looking for? Still, it was an eerie sensation to stand where the carnival used to be.

Finally, after another ten more minutes of shivering and searching, Adri sat down at the edge of the field, disappointed.

What had she expected to find? Skeletons wearing T-shirts with the names Catherine and Beezie? A crystal ball Professor Spero had left behind? It was funny, the things that lasted. Coke cans, glass, wire fences, rocks. The wind tugged at the hair that poked out beneath her hat.

"It had to be a hoax, huh? The Electric?" she said to Lily, who came and sat down beside her, pulling her teddy bear hat down tightly over her ears.

"Oh yeah." Lily nodded. "Of course."

She fiddled with the metal top of one of the Coke cans.

"They all let each other down."

"But people forgive each other. It's like a dance," Lily said.

"I wish I knew how to do that dance," Adri replied.

"Oh," Lily shook her head. "I don't think it's that you can't do it. I think you're thinking the whole thing is a *lose-lose.* Like, what if someone actually likes you? That causes *all* sorts of problems. Then each time you see them, you have to try and *keep* them. And then even if you manage that, you lose. You end up losing. Even if you go through all the work of accepting someone and occasionally looking like a fool in front of them and then figuring out if they can accept you and you can forgive each other for everything you screw up, you lose them eventually."

Lily looked at her, her bear ears flapping in the breeze. "That's why I think you don't dance, Adri. I don't think it's that you don't know the steps."

Adri held her arms around herself, shivering.

"Do you think I can change?" she finally asked.

Lily looked at her, curious and thoughtful. "Well," she replied, "are you dead?"

They smiled at each other, a slow unfolding.

"I'm freezing my boobs off," Lily said.

Driving home, Adri thought about what Lily had said at the archives. Maybe she *had* let herself worry about Catherine and Beezie and Lenore because they couldn't know or hurt her in return. But she *was* hurt. By how they had let one another down, and now their stories had vanished.

She thought about the night Catherine and Ellis had walked the same road home from the Ragbag Fair that they were driving now, trying to forgive each other. Her mind wandered to the wooden box, how Ellis had hidden it under his bed, always scared of things that were long past him. The following morning, it was still on her mind.

It was just another place she hadn't looked, nothing promising. There was no reason there'd be anything important there. But the next morning Adri pulled a blanket over her shoulders and walked downstairs and outside.

She'd never ventured into the old bunkhouse—it was barely a building anymore. She hovered outside the door for a moment, then crossed into the darkness. It smelled like dirt and old hay. There was a wooden frame where a bed used to be, the slats now broken and caved in, the room full of webs and dark corners.

She made her way through the sticky webs, knelt beside the broken bed, and ran her hands underneath it.

She felt a slit in the earth, and brushed off the dirt to reveal the two loose planks, and pulled that off to reveal a small space, just a foot wide. The wooden box was still there—though it felt like it shouldn't be, like something from a dream.

She opened the top and removed the contents slowly: a framed, grainy, black-and-white photo of a woman and her daughters. She knew them immediately: Beth—stern and proud, Catherine looking off at something to the side—an even-featured, quiet-looking kind of person but restless even as a still life—and Beezie, a hellcat for sure, with an enormous hungry grin on her face like she wanted to swallow whoever was taking the picture. Beneath it, there was a bracelet woven out of straw, half disintegrated. And beneath that, letters. Adri lost her breath.

The top one was thick, nearly bursting from its envelope, written to Beth Godspeed from Lenore Allstock, and postmarked *May 2, 1920, Cherbourg, France.* The others were in a bundle, tied together with twine, and addressed to Ellis Parrish from Catherine Godspeed, who hadn't died in the dust at all.

LENORE

PART 2

APRIL 30, 1920

Dear Beth,

There's so much to write, and I feel as if I need to write it all in one place or I'll never write any of it. I hope you're settled in somewhere to read this.

It's been ten months since that terrible day I was supposed to board the ship, and I never heard from you after the telegram I sent that day, and I don't blame you. But there are things that I need you need to know. They all involve you, whether you want them to or not. Just like when I pushed my bloody hand onto your knee, you're stuck with me, in so many ways that you didn't ask for.

The first thing I need to tell you is that I'm going to have a baby.

The second is this: that I don't know how many ways I can apologize and have it mean enough.

I've spent so much time since that day trying to figure out what went wrong. I know how angry you must be. I know that you waited for me all these years, or at least I hope you did. And then I didn't come. I know you were counting on me.

I still don't understand it completely myself. But here's my attempt to explain.

The morning I was supposed to board the Cunard, I swear I didn't have a thought in my mind about turning back. I got to Southampton early and waited in line like everyone else. I'd already said my good-byes, and while my sisters and brothers and parents were insisting I'd be back—in my mind I was already gone.

It was a foggy morning—stepping out of the train into the city, I could swear I smelled the North Sea already. The gulls were circling, the breeze was soft, and it all felt so exciting. I stood on the docks with my ticket along with the rest of the crowd, and the line moved along slowly. There was a crowd of people protesting, circling with picket signs and shouting about poison in the air. I couldn't hear myself think for all the noise.

I stepped up to the edge of the gangway just like the person did before me. I handed over my ticket to the porter. That's when I was overcome with terror. And I knew immediately that I couldn't do it. I couldn't get on.

My hands shook and the world swayed and the porter took my arm, so it must have looked like I was about to fall over. The only way I could force myself to walk was to walk away, out of the crowd and away from the ship. I rushed toward the taxi stand, and I swear I couldn't breathe, and I kept unlacing the belt of my dress, but it didn't help.

All this is a long and overdone way of saying that I was too afraid to come—too afraid of going down like the *Lusitania* or of getting to America and not finding what I came for or . . . I don't know what. That's the awful and humiliating truth. And I'm sorry I couldn't send anything but a telegram to let you know. I didn't know what to say. I didn't want to write until I could say something intelligible, and I suppose I still haven't.

I know you're disappointed in me. But believe me, you couldn't be any more disappointed than I am in myself. For all my anger with James for not staring death in the face by fighting in the war, I couldn't even get on a boat.

I'm so tired, Beth. For now, I'm going to bed, and I will write more in the morning.

MORNING, MAY 1, 1920

It seems like every time I think things will settle down and life will stand still for a while, something shifts. And the things I get so scared of aren't the ones that actually end up happening; other things come along.

I don't want to get ahead of myself. I'll explain, though even writing this is making me so tired.

For weeks after I got back from Southampton I walked around in a daze. My parents were happy to have me home, of course, instead of far away with you. But I think most of all, they wanted me to be happy—and Mother kept coming to my room to stroke my hair and chat, to try to get me interested in things. She started having her friends over for cards and dinners again, and getting involved in the business—sticking her nose in the ledgers and asking Dad to fill her in on his days at the office.

She'd started taking regular day trips to London, to shop and to sightsee, and a few times she talked me into going with her. Looking back now, I think I was thinking of James the whole time. Hoping I'd spot him. But London is a big place, and nothing came of it.

One afternoon I walked down to the cottage. I half expected and half hoped for him to still be there. I walked up quietly so I could take him by surprise, but I didn't need to. It's funny how quickly a house can go back to feeling abandoned. Some sticks and leaves had fallen in so the floor was covered in debris. A portion of the roof had already crumbled. And it looked like the spiders had moved back in. It was obvious he hadn't been there in weeks, maybe since the night I told him to leave.

And I should have felt vindicated and glad. But I didn't.

Life got back to normal. I went on my little trips with Mother and worked long hours at the factory office and went for walks. I was already getting happier, even then.

I guess people are right when they say that time helps grief. I don't agree that it heals, but maybe it wraps our losses up deeper and deeper inside so we can get on with being alive. I started having fun going to films and lying in the pasture with my books.

This went on well into the winter, falling into a routine—work, home, London. Along the way I convinced myself that I never really wanted to go to America anyway. And if I'm honest about the lies I told myself, Beth, I also decided that you were never that good of a friend to me. I listed the examples in my head of how you'd let me down. It went on like this for months.

And just when I least expected it, everything changed again.

Whenever we went to London, we always took the train to South Kensington, which is close to the British Museum. Of course, it always made me think of James and his imaginary famous family. I'd even go linger out in front of the museum while Mother went to a fitting or some other time-consuming appointment. I'd stand there and picture all those shells and bones inside, but never go inside. I'd imagine the people James had spun in my head. It felt like a memory or a dream full of light.

It was an afternoon in early May when I saw him. I was standing there looking up at the windows when I decided it was idiotic to loiter there on the steps without going inside. He was right there in the main hall standing beside a towering stuffed elephant. He had a big box in his arms and was discussing the weather with a security guard. He stood tall, confidently, as if his scars were invisible now, even to him.

I stood there bewildered and on the verge of ducking outside again when he turned around and saw me.

Then he very politely came up to me and reached to shake my hand.

"Lenore," he said. I didn't like that he didn't call me Allstock.

He was so composed, and I was not. "What brings you to the museum?" he asked politely, not a trace of the past in his voice. He'd gotten past it.

"What are you doing here?" I sputtered back.

"Oh." He looked down at the box in his arms. "Getting ready."

"Ready for what?"

"I'm going away," he said brightly. "To Indonesia. Remember?"

"Oh?"

"Our funding's been approved."

"How long will you be gone?" I asked, trying to hide my confusion. Because of course, I'd always thought it was all a lie.

He seemed to falter a bit at that, and it was the first and only indication that it bothered him to see me.

"Five years," he said with a smile and a wince, as if to apologize. "We'd like to stay long enough to make it worthwhile."

"The museum closes to the public in ten," the guard said gently to the room, giving us a quick sideways glance.

We stood there looking at each other in awkward silence, and I was about to make my excuses to go when he smiled at me.

"Want to meet my parents?"

As you may have guessed already, Beth, probably faster than I did, his parents are famous naturalists, just like he said. He took me back into the dusty offices of the museum and introduced me. His father is short with glasses, and his mother has curly brown hair and sharp hazel eyes and looks like him. It was strange to see a version of his face without anything getting in its way.

They were both friendly, and their conversation was bright and lively. They said things like "Oh, so this is Lenore" as if they'd heard a lot about me but not anything about the falling out.

And then, though the museum had closed, James asked me if I wanted to see the exhibit his family had been working on all these years, and we went and wandered down a dimly lit hall of taxidermied rodents and rare shells and rocks.

I think a year ago I would have found it the most boring section of the museum, but with James's enthusiasm it all looked fascinating and . . . I can't explain it . . . like it all meant so much more than at first glance. It was like underneath all these silly little shells was this long thread of time. With James talking me through it, it felt like a story about people.

Finally it was late and I needed to get back to Mother, so he walked me to the front steps. I'll never forget what the river looked like, how the sun was sparkling on it, and he shook my hand and then hugged me, and we said good-bye.

"So they're not going to shoot you?" I teased, trying to make light of things.

He shook his head. "No one's come after me yet. I don't think anyone has the heart," he said, waving a hand toward his face, his body. "Soon I'll be gone anyway."

"When?" I asked, lingering.

"Tuesday."

"Well, I'll think of you that day." I shook his hand again. "I'm glad I met you, James," I said firmly. "And good luck."

"Good luck," he repeated.

I wanted to thank him, and I didn't know for what. For helping me to say good-bye to my brother in some way I still can't understand. I couldn't find the words.

And I walked away along the river.

I didn't think that I'd ever see him again.

Don't you think, Beth, that it's easy to judge people for their sadness when it hasn't happened to you? To see it as too strange, or too big, or not done in the right way, until you've felt the monster of it inside you? I think that is one thing I've learned, and I think it's made me better.

And on that note, I've been holed up in bed with this letter all morning and have to go eat. I'll try to write again tonight.

I left you at the Thames.

I'll start back in Forest Row.

That night, back at home, I stayed up late reading. I'd unearthed *The Blue Fairy Book* and was on "The History of Jack the Giant-Killer" that you always thought was too violent . . . while I'd pretend I was Jack, slaying everyone in sight. Memories were buzzing in my head of when we were little, but not in a sad way. I had this pleasant feeling: happy those times had happened, even though they were over.

I had my window open, and I put down my book when I

smelled the chimney smoke on the air. It wasn't coming from our house. Even at that first moment, I had a tiny bit of hope.

I put on my shoes in the hall and walked outside. A few stars were out, so I gazed up for a bit, then ventured into the woods. And sure enough, there was firelight blazing deep in the woods. The smoke was coming from the cottage.

I was so scared it would be someone else—a passerby or a camper using the fireplace—but he looked up and smiled as I entered.

"I was hoping you'd see it and come," he said. "Otherwise I was going to come throw pebbles at your window or something." We stared at each other for a while without saying anything. Then he leaned over the table and held up a plate with a small half of a chicken on it. "I brought dinner."

We sat on the leaf-and-twig-strewn floor and ate. At first the conversation was slow—I asked him to tell me the details of the trip, and he gave me all the formalities: the route he would take, the size of the crew, how they got the funding. The distance between us made my chest ache, but slowly we both relaxed.

He showed me a new Eveready torchlight he'd bought for the voyage, and we kept turning it on and off, lighting up the room and then watching it go dark.

"Lumbering into the woods to piss will never be the same," he joked.

We both got quiet.

"Did she end things with you before or after . . . ?"

"After . . ." He looked down at his hands. "But it wasn't her fault. Who could live with this?" he asked. "Who'd want to build a life with this?" By the gentle way he said it, I wondered if he was still in love with her, and I decided he probably was.

I cleared my throat.

"I'm sorry, James," I said simply. I knew I didn't need to say why.

He looked at me long and hard. "I'm sorry too, Lenore," he replied. "So sorry I lied to you. Sorry I wasn't brave. I'm not one of those people who things are ever clear to, like you are. And I'm sorry for that too, I guess."

"It's not that great, being too decided."

"But it's powerful."

I didn't know what else to say. I think the conversation would have died there if he hadn't suddenly widened his eyes and stood up.

"I almost forgot. I brought you something."

He stepped outside for a moment, leaving me curious, and then came back holding something out toward me pressed carefully between his palms. He squatted before me, and I had to lean closer to see what it was he was cupping so carefully in his hands.

It was small and compact, yellow and green, pretty as a jewel. And it was moving. A tiny head shifted, a pair of tiny eyes looked around, curious.

"My parents brought her back. She's from the Galapagos—these islands, very remote. One of the great last wildernesses on

Earth. I can't take care of her now that I'm leaving." He held her out to me, and as I opened my hands he slid her very gently into them. Her shell was smooth, and her head tickled my hands as it darted in and out of her shell.

"I thought I might give her to you. Will you take care of her?"

I cupped the little life in my hands, and even though she was only a reptile, I liked her immediately.

"I have a little bowl for her. But she'll need a bigger space as she grows," he said. "I have to warn you, she'll get rather big. You don't have to take her."

"I'll guard her with my life," I said.

I've been sitting here for almost an hour, and I can't bring myself to write the rest. I can't explain myself, or him, or maybe I don't want to explain. We aren't in love, that much I know for sure. But we do love each other.

The only thing I can say is that war has made us different, Beth. We want so much. We know our lives are only here for right now. I don't know how else to explain what happened between us—all of it—from building a house out of sticks to how knowing James helped me let go of Teddy to our last night at the cottage and what happened between us then—except that maybe we wanted to live our lives as much as we possibly could, and for a little while it felt like we were. And now he's gone to find his dreams. And I have no regrets, even though maybe I'm supposed to.

So here I am. I never sleep. My belly is already getting big, but it is still small enough to hide. The baby is moving—every once in a while I feel a movement against my skin, but by the time I put my hand there, it's stopped. I can't imagine it. I can't fathom there's a human in there.

I have two more things to tell you and then I'll finish. And both of them may shock you even more than what's shocked you already.

I keep thinking of my old broken bones, from that terrible fall off the barn when we were kids. One of the bones, you may remember, was my sacrum, in my pelvis. Now it haunts me. What if I can't deliver this baby? To be honest I don't know if I'm more scared for her or me. All I know is that either way, I need you with me.

And this brings me to my second and final shocking thing. I suppose it won't be so shocking when you see the postmark on the letter. I plan to mail this from our next stop, so maybe you'll already know by the time you open it that I'm writing this from the belly of a ship. I didn't tell you before I left because I didn't want to lie twice. I wanted to make sure I'd get it right.

I've been writing to the endless rocking rhythm of the ocean. And I'm surprised to find that being here isn't scary at all.

I have everything planned. Once I land in New York, I know how I'll make my way out to Wichita by train. I already know your address; that was your first mistake. You can't escape me now.

My parents hate the idea of course, but they couldn't stop

me. And the baby is my secret—yours and mine. When this thing comes along to change my life, I want to be with you when it happens.

James was always right, that our friendship is complicated, but I'll never love anyone half as much as I love you, Beth.

We reach Cherbourg tomorrow, and I'll mail this letter then.

Love, Lenore

CATHERINE

PART 2

AUGUST 3, 1934

Dear Ellis,

It's been three days since we left Canaan, and already I feel like I'd give anything to see our dead garden again, or Galapagos craning her neck at me from across the yard.

We're camped in the woods on the edge of a town called Bonner Springs, just outside of Kansas City (where I hope to mail this letter), far away from the road so no one will see us. We have some bread, jerky, two potatoes, and two dollars. We have one wool blanket to share, which Beezie has stolen in her sleep. Tomorrow we'll walk toward downtown and hope to catch another ride close in.

We are headed for New York.

I know that above anything else I owe you in this letter, I owe you an apology. I'm sorry that I couldn't bring myself to say good-bye to you. I know I snuck us out of Canaan like thieves in the night. I never dreamt that, between you and me, I'd be the leaver and not the left. And I hope one day you'll understand that it took all my courage just to go, with none left to tell you I was going.

Our first morning, we managed to hitch a ride from a wealthy couple in a brand-new Buick outside Canaan. Two more rides and long hours of walking have brought us this far since. I'll never forget the shock of that first morning.

What we saw in the hundred miles we rode that day made my heart sink. Town after town, mile after mile, we passed emptiness and desolation—the ground stripped up and blown away, the acres rolling and featureless like the heart of a desert. Mama used to say that when she arrived in Kansas it was bluestem and birds as far as you could see.

It was treacherous and slow, with dust drifts covering the roads in many places and dirt coating the windshield. At times our driver had to stick his head out the window just to see. We felt lucky though, as we drove past people who were stranded, their cars shorted out or their wagons stuck in the dirt.

It always felt like Canaan was in the eye of the storms that were suffocating us. But driving those miles, I finally understood we have only been a speck in a desert of loss. Ellis, they say it's us who have torn up the land. If that's true, how could we have such power to destroy? And can we ever fix it?

I don't know what turned my steps east instead of west, after slipping Beezie out of bed and packing our few things and making it past you and Mama and the end of the drive and town with her on my back—or why I stood on one side of the road to look for a ride instead of the other. I like to think it's some inner compass, telling me the way I need to go. But I think probably it was an impulse, and nothing to do with which way was right.

The whole time I stood there, I was so near turning back I started retracing my steps home, hobbling back the way we'd come, already defeated.

And then the Buick appeared in the distance and slowed to a stop in front of us.

And a minute later, we were gone.

Beezie hasn't forgiven me for taking her. At the time she was too groggy to know what was happening. Now she doesn't understand I had no choice. I suppose you and Mama won't understand either.

We heard this morning that the world hasn't ended back home but that it's come close, and that the other night Kansas had the storm to end all storms. They say the dust reached ten thousand feet in the air, and the haze stretched all the way to New York and three hundred miles out to sea, dusting the ships like rain. Here, we could only see a haze floating over the sun.

The only thing that keeps me going is my hope that Beezie will get better and Kansas will get better, and that I'll make it back to you. Though I don't know if I will, and I don't know if you'll wait.

I hope you got the letter I left outside your door—it is from Lenore to Mama. I hope it explains some things I couldn't say before I left. There were more, but those were about Mama and Lenore before me, and I left them for her to keep for herself. I left them on the kitchen table and then on second thought, I left my journal too. She'll know about us now, and I hope it doesn't cause problems for you. But I don't care for keeping secrets anymore.

Trust in me, you said, the other night. *Let me save you.*

But it's clear now that you can't save us, and Mama can't save us, and God won't save us, and the Electric won't save us.

So we have to try and save ourselves.

P.S. Please tell Mama we are all right. I'm too angry to write to her, and I imagine she's too angry to want to hear from me.

Love, Catherine

AUGUST 5, 1934

Dear Ellis,

It's taken two days of walking and catching rides to make it to Harrisburg. Mostly, when we're not riding, I carry Beezie on my back. I count our money every night, and it's never enough.

Today we crossed paths with a group of travelers who overlapped us like a big galaxy swirling around a little one—we shared news and a little food and then parted ways. People are drifting all over the country, crisscrossing each other—carrying suitcases, camped beside the road, or sleeping in their cars. We're homesick all the time, but we've decided we can't get enough of the miles and miles of lush green pine trees. We've seen ugly and beautiful things—an airplane pulling an ad that said *Smoke Lucky Strike Cigarettes,* misty hills and fog-filled lakes that look like they're out of a fairy tale.

The thing I hate to see is the way people look at us—like we're carrying something they don't want to catch.

• • •

Last night, Beezie took me by surprise.

"How are you going to marry Ellis if he's in Canaan and we're in New York?" she asked. She always picks up on more than you think she does.

"What makes you think I'd marry him?" I said.

She had a coughing fit after that, but it didn't deter her. "I don't want you to end up an old maid," she said as soon as she could breathe again. "All alone."

"I'm not alone. I'm with you, aren't I?" I said.

"Doesn't count."

"Of course it counts."

"Not if you're an old maid."

I gave up. As you know all too well, you can't win an argument with Beezie.

She's wheezing beside me now, in her sleep. I always know exactly where she is because of that whistling sound in her chest that fills me with dread. I've taken her out of the dust, but that hasn't taken the dust out of her.

All day all I think about is taking care of Beezie, and whether this will help her, and I only let my mind wander to other things after she falls asleep—mostly to you and to Mama and Lenore.

The more I think, the more I wonder who am I if I'm not Mama's and the farm's, and the girl who's always been hoping to be yours? I'm trying to find out. And I'm sorry to be so blunt, and to tell you about you and me as if it weren't you I was talking to. But you are the only person I can show myself to, Ellis. You always made my rough edges feel real.

It's strange, but what makes me angriest with Mama is not that she lied to me and that all this time I had a mother I didn't even know about (though I can't think of Mama as anything but Mama, even now, and it's hard to think how Lenore was my mother too, though I know it's true). What hurts me worse is how Mama abandoned her and tried to pull her down when they were kids. I wonder more than anything whether, when the woman who gave me life showed up with me in her belly, was Mama happy to see her? It seems to make all the difference, whether or not she loved her in the end.

Where are you sitting while you read this? Do you still think I've made a mistake? Are you angry with me? Do you want to forget me? I wonder these things all the time.

Love, Catherine

AUGUST 6, 1934

Tomorrow, it happens. I'm breathless and maybe more scared than I've ever been by any duster. If all goes well, we'll arrive in New York by walking across the George Washington Bridge. I'm so scared and excited and hopeful and terrified my hands are shaking as I write. What will we find when we get there?

For the last night of our journey I'm sitting here with only our campfire and the big black sky and the millions of stars to keep me company.

Tomorrow feels like flipping a coin. Every moment I wonder

if I've done the right thing, but tomorrow we begin to find out, and I almost can't stand the thought of that.

We've seen so many other people trailing in the same direction as we are, cars packed to the gills. I want to have hope for them too, but in my mind, I'm ruthless. I want other people to survive, but I want Beezie to survive more. I want to think that I'm special and Beezie is special and that whoever is up there, if anyone is, has His eye on us . . . and that we'll make it even if other people don't. I want Beezie to be the lucky one. I am so selfish for her welfare I think I could smother anyone who got in the way, and I know that's evil, and yet I can't feel any other way.

I'll mail this from the road tomorrow if I can. And I'll write again when I can tell you whether New York is going to save or sinks us. I won't write until I know for sure.

I think it would be too easy, otherwise, to get turned back once we are there. I think now is the time I need to put you and home behind me, if I'm to make any go of it at all.

Love, Catherine

JANUARY 15, 1935

Dear Ellis,

It's been almost six months since I last saw you, and five since I wrote, and I think this may be the last letter I ever send to you. After so much time, I wonder if you think of me as much as I think of you. And I wonder if you do, what you think. Are you still waiting for me or have you let me go? I think time works differently depending on where you are, and whether you're the leaver or the left, so I can't assume I know.

I'm sitting against the living room radiator in an old apartment on the Lower East Side of Manhattan. My face and hands are freezing, but my back feels like it's on fire. Still, I can't bring myself to pull away from the heat.

The room is shared with five other people, Okies like me. It's cramped, shabby, and cold—with peeling paint and mice scrabbling up and down behind the walls.

It's not where I expected to be, and there's so much that has changed, and so many things have happened, and some are harder to write than others. I think this whole time, I've been trying to keep my promise to you and myself, of waiting until I could say that yes I'm coming home, or no, I'm not. But until now, it's been hard to make out what's ahead of me, and at first, the days were just too full to think straight.

It rained the entire first week we arrived in Manhattan, but it was good luck for us. So few people were out in the downpour that I was the first to reply to a *Help Wanted* sign that was posted at a local laundry. (Jobs are so hard to come by here.) By asking around I rented a spot in this apartment that same night—just a section of the living room, really, shared with three other people separated by sheets—and have lived here ever since.

From that day on, I worked every day all day until I wanted to fall down (and you know I'm used to work). Meanwhile, Beezie didn't get better . . . she got worse.

As soon as we were settled, I spent what little money we had to take her to a doctor at Mercy Hospital. He barely had to look at her to tell me the problem: that the dust had damaged her lungs so much that they couldn't flush the bad things out. That's why even though we'd left home, she was still as bad as ever.

He told me that with time, they could heal, but to watch for fever because that would mean infection. He said if that happened to rush her to him right away. The only thing we could do in the meantime was give her rest, and food, and air—none of which are all that easy to come by here.

When I wrote to Mama that night—just one quick letter, nothing more—to tell her where we were and that we were okay and to ask her to pass that on to you, I didn't tell her what the doctor said. I don't know, now, looking back, if that was the right choice or not. I didn't apologize either. My anger was still too sharp; it outweighed my guilt for leaving. Then again, if she'd known we were leaving she never would have let us go.

Those first weeks, the thing that shocked us most about the city was the absence of the sky. You can't see it unless you make a point of looking for it—maybe you remember that. Even right now I'm looking out my window at bricks. For someone who grew up with an endless view, it still unsettles me. And I can't get used to the grayness.

But there are good things too: in place of space there is endless electricity. So many lights you'd think we were living in a constellation. And theaters, music—people gobbling life up like it was about to disappear. You can stay out all night if you want and nobody cares. You can do just about anything and nobody cares; it feels like even God can't see you. It's a place that breaks your heart and makes you giddy at the same time.

It was so cold some of those early days that I could swear my blood froze solid. I thought Kansas could be frigid, but it has nothing on the wind tunnels of the avenues. And as fall marched on into winter, Beezie got more lethargic and more sick. It drove me half-crazy having a life—the dearest life I know—balanced in my hands like that, with no one else to lean on. It was like hot coals in my stomach all the time.

Whenever Beezie was at her worst, I talked her through it by talking us to Canaan. I'd describe the day we'd get to go home, riding down the highway, or maybe on a train first class if we were lucky and suddenly, inexplicably rich . . . walking around the bend of Jericho Road that leads to the first sight of the house. In real life I'd take her for walks by the Hudson River to breathe the air until our faces were so cold they felt like they'd fall off.

The truth is that from the first, New York didn't feel like where we were supposed to be. "It's not like I pictured," Beezie pointed out one of those afternoons. "We're not sparkly here."

I laughed and said that didn't make sense. But I do believe, now, that places change you, and that while the city was lit up all around us, we were growing flatter and smaller by the day.

"We need Mama," Beezie said.

I couldn't forgive Mama enough to agree yet. I'd think about

Lenore, who'd loved me and loved Mama too.

And then I lost my job, by falling asleep on my feet after a long night comforting Beezie. I couldn't find another one after that—too many desperate people wanting the same thing. I cried the first time we waited on a breadline. It was both the humiliation and my sinking realization that the city was defeating us.

I began to plan our trip home.

But that's when we met Sofia Ortiz.

LATER—

She swept into our rat-infested apartment one morning with a suitcase and her chin lifted up like she was walking into a palace. She had hair as short as a boy's, and a bag full of clothes, and nothing else, but it was like she owned everything in sight.

"Sofia," she introduced herself, giving me and then Beezie a handshake that could break bones. She'd just arrived in the city and rented a corner of the room, which she decorated with anything—sticks she found in the park, pieces of junk from the street—and made it something like home.

She threw herself into cleaning the entire apartment, even the areas that belonged to other people. Instead of annoying everyone, it won them over. When one of our apartment mates asked her why she'd cut her hair so short, she said simply, "It was in the way," and blew a breath at her bangs. Then she disappeared for hours at a time, and she came back one afternoon with a job at a stable uptown.

She'd often try to help people around the house, offering advice, giving them her undivided attention, talking politics, sharing the news from the papers with people who didn't read, or who only read Spanish. It was Sofia who first told us about the government projects they were doing back home, buying back big parts of the plains and reseeding them with grass, showing farmers how to plant to keep the soil in place like it used to be.

After that we would see her come and go, but with all of us so busy surviving (I was down to almost nothing of my shrinking savings), we didn't really talk until one night, when Beezie coughed for hours without letting up.

Sofia emerged from her sheets, disheveled and, I thought, annoyed, and disappeared into the kitchen. When she returned she had a metal bowl full of hot, steaming water in her hands.

"Can I?" she asked, her hair standing up all over the place and her face still smushed from sleep. I nodded.

She knelt by Beezie and unrolled a blanket from under her arm and laid it over Beezie's head like a tent, putting the bowl of hot water underneath.

"Breathe," she said, and Beezie did, sucking in air, pushing it out in rattling bursts. "Try to breathe as deeply as you can."

Beezie began to breathe more slowly and grow calmer.

"I'll be right back," Sofia said. She returned with a little brown bag, pulled out a small jar of some kind of spice and another jar of honey, and poured a little of the hot water out into a tin mug, mixing it all together.

"Saffron helps," she said.

"Are you a doctor?" I asked. Though she was young like me, she moved with the confidence of someone who knew everything.

Her hands worked in her bag, going through this and that jar as she looked for what she needed. "I'm a veterinarian," she said, giving me a rueful smile. "I'm a lot of things."

Beezie had calmed down by this point, and her breath was coming clearer, and Sofia pulled the tent off of her head.

"Beezie? Can I listen to you?"

"Yes," I said quickly, and Beezie widened her eyes at me accusingly as Sofia put her stethoscope to her chest, then pulled back and put her hand on her forehead. Before Beezie could protest she pulled up her shirt and slapped a mustard pack across the middle of her rib cage.

For a moment Beezie poked and prodded it with her fingers, deciding whether or not to be outraged, I suppose, and then she leaned against me, exhausted.

Sofia sat with us in companionable silence as I rocked her.

"Thank you," I said quietly, and she shrugged. She cocked her head toward Beezie, then back at me.

"The congestion . . . she's full of dust," she said, only half a question.

I nodded.

She shook her head. "The little ones—they get it the worst. It's a good reason to leave. So many good reasons. I can give you some of this—saffron, mustard. They help. You can try garlic soup too," she added. "But really, these are mostly home remedies." She leaned forward and tousled Beezie's hair. "She should go back to the doctor," she said.

"We can't afford it," I said. "I don't have a job."

"I'll find you one," Sofia said simply. I couldn't make out if she was truly so confident or really just good at pretending. I've never met someone so talented at making life submit to her.

Beezie had fallen asleep against me, her warm red cheek against my chest, with long troubled breaths. I know it sounds strange, but in those difficult days, I wrapped myself up in the tiniest things about her, because I felt always on the verge of losing her: the complexity and intricacy of her fingers in my own hands, the beautiful length of her lashes, her rattly laugh. It hypnotized me, listening to her and knowing that for those moments, she was okay.

Sofia told us her story: her family had farmed sheep in Texas, on the prairie—they hadn't ripped up their prairie grass but the dust, indiscriminate, had buried them all the same, and their sheep had died.

"And then people started saying we should go back to Mexico. My father was born in Texas. It made no sense." Her eyes were big, remembering. "Things fell apart. We lost the farm to the bank and we lost . . . other things you can never get back. My mom and my two brothers went to south Texas to look for work. I chose east."

"You're a strong person," I said. "Much stronger than me."

Sofia shook her head. "You become as strong as you have to

be, don't you think? When you're trying to protect someone you love, you'll do anything. Try any little trick that could possibly work, even if it's just garlic soup. Walk your feet right off your legs. It's just what people do."

She studied Beezie on my lap and ran a hand gently across the top of Beezie's head. "I know all the home remedies because I know about dust," she finally said. "I know about willing someone to breathe and wishing you could breathe for them. And saying anything to try to make their fear smaller, even though you can't."

The room stretched around us in silence. Sofia looked suddenly lost. It was as if, in a moment, a heaviness in her posture pulled the air out of the room.

She pulled back, straightening up. "My dad. He was an older dad; I was the youngest. He worked too hard. I think that's why the dust hit him hard, too."

I waited for her to go on.

Sofia smiled sadly. "He was the kind of person who never sat back. He was always eager to learn the next thing, he was always tinkering with something, always something in his hands—a book or a piece of machinery or an animal he was tending to—he wanted to figure it out. He told me, 'If I waste time I might as well be dead.' He believed hard work always paid off, and that if you were good to people, they'd be good back to you. The dust . . ." she said, shrugging, "changed that."

She tapped her fingertips against one another, looking at

her hands. "Growing up, he pushed me more than he did my brothers . . . with school, with business, and everything. He saw something in me, I think, similar to him. He wanted me to leave town, to make something big of myself. He didn't care what, just as long as it was more than being a farmer or a farmer's wife.

"When he . . ." Sofia blinked up at the ceiling. I touched her hand to let her know she didn't have to say the words, that I knew she was saying she had lost him. I tried not to think about what that meant about Beezie.

"After he was gone, I didn't know what I wanted; it just fell into a shadow. So I followed what was inside him instead. I made my plans to come here. That was about a year ago, now, that I decided. I think that's what he would have wanted."

"But it isn't what you want," I said.

Sofia tilted her head back and forth to indicate she didn't know.

"All my dad wanted was for me to have the things we didn't. But all I want is what I had. I loved watching over our farm; I loved that it was physical and mental all at once. You have to know which seeds go where, when, and which plants complement one another, and the animals; it's like a constant equation you are working out. But then, it's also something you do with your body. Something where you touch the ground. It takes all of you. I love that." She smiled. "And I like the idea of my own realm. I don't want to look at bricks." She leaned back on her hands. "But what of it? Someone else owns our farm now."

I knew this feeling, from my mom, my neighbors. You could love a place as if it were a living thing.

"I was never a very spiritual person," Sofia said. "But I pray to him. I keep asking him to lead me and help me. I don't know. Maybe it's foolish, but I feel he's here."

She studied Beezie, then me. "I'll make you a pact, okay? I like you, and I think you like me. I saw Beezie and . . . it just makes me feel close to my father, to help, or at least to try. And we've got no one else. So we'll be there for each other. If you think I'm so strong, you can rely on me. And I'll do the same. We are homeless now, our families are far away. Why not have each other?"

I felt like she was rescuing me, because I couldn't imagine she could need me half as much as I needed her. I could only nod, too overcome to speak.

We didn't say good night until close to dawn. But by the time Sofia and I were done talking that morning, I believed I could survive another week in New York.

NEXT DAY—

One week turned into two, and two into three. Sofia made good on her promise to get me a job—this time at a garment factory along the river. But we didn't flourish like she did. People at the stables began to request her by name. She had more work than she knew what to do with. She sometimes worked all night, out on an emergency or a birth at the stables, and would tiptoe in at dawn, nearly falling over with exhaustion. But every time she walked into the apartment she lit the rest of us up.

She was unlike anyone I'd ever met—or ever would have if I hadn't left Canaan. And having her with us helped me miss home a little less.

We found a mattress and dragged it up the stairs for me and Beezie to sleep on. We started to feel a little more at home, and to let ourselves enjoy things a little.

One afternoon all three of us went to Coney Island and ate until we wanted to burst and then rode a Ferris wheel. Beezie threw up all over me, but it was worth it. We put our feet in the ocean even though it was frigid, just to say we'd done it. Beezie screamed and ran in and out of the water, and Sofia stood beside me, shivering. We stared at the waves for ages—coming in, going out.

"She's getting better?" Sofia asked.

"I don't know," I said. "It seems about the same."

"Do you think you'll go home, Cathy?" she asked. "When she *is*?"

She looked nervous, waiting for my answer. I could tell she didn't want me to go.

"I hope so." But, Ellis, at that moment the thought of going home made me shrink a bit inside. Like it was somewhere safer, but smaller than where I was.

Sofia nodded. She looked like she was trying to sort out a difficult thought. "I wonder if sometimes you can miss something so much it breaks you, and still be happy you left."

"If anything ever happened to Beezie, I don't think I'd ever want to see Canaan again," I said. "Mama would never forgive me."

"But nothing's going to happen," Sofia said. It was the one time I've ever known her to be wrong.

It wasn't long after that that things turned for Beezie. One morning, she couldn't get out of bed, and I stayed home trying all of our remedies at once. Nothing made a difference. By that night she was gasping instead of wheezing. Chest pains were making her cry. By midnight, she was delirious and sweating.

Sofia happened to be away that night for a birth. We had no one else. I hoisted Beezie onto my back, left a frantic note, and ran twenty blocks—all the way to Mercy Hospital, stumbling several times along the way.

As we walked in the doors, Beezie started to shake.

The hospital was crowded and chaotic, but I pushed my way to the front of a group at the front desk. When the receptionist saw Beezie convulsing in my arms, she called a nurse.

Beezie was terrified at that point, and flailing. She screamed for me as they tried to separate us, so I followed, my legs shaking with fear, as they rushed her down the hall. No one stopped me. They moved her to a bed and began rubbing hot cloths over her chest. When they tried to inject her with something to stop the shaking, she fought them like a wild animal.

The nurses were trying to hold her down when someone pushed into the room behind me, and I looked up to see Sofia sweeping past me, as if she'd been in the room a million times.

Beezie was too delirious to notice her, she was too busy fighting, but Sofia grabbed her hands, trying to keep her from thrashing the nurses so they could do what they needed to do.

"Beezie, how old are you?" Sofia asked, shooting me a terrified glance. "Tell me how old you are."

Beezie blinked up at her, choking for breath, angry tears streaming down her flushed cheeks.

"It's important," Sofia said, though I couldn't fathom why.

"Six," Beezie finally choked. "It hurts, Cathy!"

"I know it hurts, Beezie, but pay attention. How many fingers?" Sofia asked, holding up three and staring at Beezie evenly, massaging her hands as one of the nurses finally managed to stick a needle in her arm.

"Three," Beezie said. She was calming, her breath was rattling but also slowing, though she was still writhing in pain.

"What's your favorite flower?" Sofia demanded.

Beezie seemed to take in the room a little. She let a doctor remove her shirt, but her eyes kept coming back to Sofia and her firm, steady gaze.

"I don't know," she said, and struggled for another deep breath.

"Just think about it," Sofia said. I could see it didn't matter what the question was; she was just trying to calm her, to relax her a bit. Like she might do with an animal. I couldn't comprehend her composure; I could barely breathe myself.

"A lily," Beezie said, I think because it's one of the only

flowers she knows. Mama used to grow them, remember? But not anymore.

"I'll tell you what, Beezie," Sofia said, still massaging Beezie's hands, holding her tight. "If you let the doctors work on you, I promise I'll name my first child Lily, in honor of you."

Tears were still running down Beezie's cheeks, but she seemed distracted as they pushed more needles into her arm. It was hooked to a tube and the nurse explained it would deliver antibiotics to fight the infection.

"What if you have a son?" Beezie wheezed, after a few moments of watching the doctors fearfully.

"He'll be Mister Lily Ortiz," Sofia said.

A weak smile formed on Beezie's lips, though she kept on shivering.

"He won't have your last name though," she said. "He'll have your husband's."

Sofia's face was firm, and she brushed aside her hair. "I'll never give up my name," she said.

I'm back against the radiator again. It's late. I need to write these last few things, and now I think I'm putting it off, because I feel like if these are the last words I get to say to you, I want to say them right.

The hospital was full of people as badly off as we were, and so Sofia and I had to do most of the nursing. But it was the medicine that really mattered.

For the next three days, we stayed together. We rubbed

Beezie down constantly, boiled water for steam, and made her practically live under a tent of towels. I knew that I'd lose my job again, but there was no room for anything else.

And if there is a God, he or she or it had mercy on me, and all of my mistakes, because Beezie lived anyway.

I'll never forget that morning. I woke before dawn and padded around her bed, trying not to wake her.

I was still in a haze because I'd dreamt about home—Galapagos and the dead brown garden and Mama. So I was still half there in my head as I pulled on my clothes and combed my hair.

It wasn't until I was dressed that I noticed something wasn't right. The place where Beezie slept was silent. No wheezing, no coughing, nothing.

I let out a gasp as I swept across the room toward her. But she wasn't in her bed.

I heard her shuffle in behind me. She was holding a piece of cake she'd hornswaggled out of someone down the hall.

She was blinking at me, and smiled at my look of shock. And then she said, "You look like somebody died."

I didn't dare to write it down at first. Even now, I'm still scared to say it. It's been seven weeks since then, and every day, little by little, Beezie is getting better.

There are two things left to tell you, Ellis, and these are the hardest for me to write.

One is that I'm not coming home.

I will try to explain this to you as well as I can, but I don't know if I'll ever be able to explain it well enough.

Life has moved on since that awful day at the hospital. We've been happy and safe and deliriously lucky. We are grateful, but we've also stayed unsettled and poor.

On Sundays, Beezie and I go for walks and imagine we're as wealthy as the people we sometimes pass on the street. We tell ourselves the city is ours. I found a new job at a factory and I work six days a week, but it's barely enough to get by. And I think about money a lot. It's what blew Sofia here looking for work and what blows me every day to the factory. I suppose money is partly what powered the lights Lenore went to see in London and so many of the inventions that came before and after. Money made this city grow and bustle, and it also makes it hard. I suppose money is what turned Kansas to dust.

Beezie is made of rubber these days—or elastic. You wouldn't believe it if you saw her—how much she's recovered. These days she glows brighter than that ball of light I made her touch.

Part of it is that two weeks ago, she and I got the biggest surprise of our lives. One you must already know of.

The bell had been ringing for a good three minutes, and I was trying to wrestle Beezie into her clothes. A woman we live with was the one who answered it and came upstairs with someone behind her.

"You have a visitor," she said, and Beezie screamed as if it were a monster and not Mama standing on the landing with her suitcase clutched in both hands. She was such an apparition I nearly fainted myself.

For the first time since she got them, Mama has left her precious Galapagos and her precious farm behind. She's surprised us by coming after us.

Beezie stuck herself onto her like a slug and has barely peeled herself off since.

Of course, we were eager for news of home, and of you, and that's all we talked about at first.

I asked about you first, once we'd gotten over the initial shock, and the explanations of her arrival and how she'd come.

Mama looked reluctant to speak, and I knew afterward she must have read my journal like I meant her to, or maybe she had known how I felt about you all along.

She said you moved into town. She said you work at Jack's. And that you promised to take care of Galapagos as long as she's away. Of course, I knew instantly what you working at Jack's could mean.

"I think he's angry with you, Cathy," she said. "And Lyla's a good girl. And he knows that. Her dad gave him a job." She took a deep breath and let it out. "I think he's waiting to see what you do."

I nodded. I tried to let the jealousy settle over me all at once. Still, even right now, I am jealous of so many things. I'm jealous of the things you touch, and the blankets you sleep under, I'm jealous of Jack who gets to see you, and of course so jealous of Lyla.

"I feel sorry for that girl," Mama added.

"Why?"

Mama gave me a look. "She can't erase you."

I hope this is true, Ellis, and I also don't.

We didn't talk about Lenore at first. But one night after Beezie was in bed, Mama followed me onto the front stoop of the building. We sat side by side and watched people going past. For a while I was too nervous to speak, and my anger, in the reality of Mama's presence, has dribbled away. Mama broke the silence instead.

"I didn't plan for it to be a secret," she began, as if we were in the middle of a conversation we've been having for months. "At first you were so young, and then you lost your dad, and I didn't want to add this other loss too. And then I just got scared, the longer it went. There were things I regretted about her and me, that I couldn't put into words. And I couldn't tell you about her without them."

I rubbed my palms together slowly, back and forth, looking down on the street.

"What do you want to ask me?" she said. "I'll tell you anything you want to know."

I thought for a long time. "Why did you stop writing her?" I said. It was strangely the thing I wanted to know more than anything else. "Didn't you love her anymore?"

Mama, as if exhausted, leaned back against the wall, her brown hair falling in wisps around her face, a little disheveled but still tidy.

"You have to understand," she began haltingly. "Lenore was brave, and a bit intolerant, and a bit impatient. She didn't like weakness, especially in herself. But she always stood up for me. She was bold, dazzling. She was a hero to me, larger than life."

She sighed, and she seemed to want to stop there. She looked at me for a moment, and then went on. "I looked up to her and idolized her. I think half the reason I got engaged so fast was so she'd think I was having this exciting life in America, when really I was lost without her. All that time I was so homesick, but I'd never tell her that." She shook her head. "I don't know why. I don't know why, when we were kids, I had to tell her everything that was wrong with her . . . and always had to act like I had something figured out that she didn't. It's like I wanted to pull her back to my level—the level of the small, scared person I could be. I didn't want her to find out I couldn't keep up. Even when she was grieving, it felt like she was going through something more important than I could ever grasp. That's how big she was in my mind."

"I understand," I said bitterly. "You were jealous of her."

"No." Mama shook her head, her mouth tightening. "Not jealous. I didn't want to be left behind." She laid her face against her hands for a moment and then pulled back. "It's strange, isn't it, how we can push people away because we want to be near them? Isn't that the silliest thing?" She smiled ruefully. "All these years trying to change it, and I've still been a timid person. What I should have done for Beezie . . . and let you do instead . . ."

"You're here now," I said.

She looked away and shook her head. "I hadn't gotten the letters from the ship, you know, before Lenore arrived. So when she showed up on my doorstep, her pregnancy just beginning to show, it was a complete shock. It was May, but she was shivering from head to toe. You could have knocked me over with a feather." Her smile grew, and a tear ran down the side of her nose.

"She didn't even ask me for reasons. She just said, 'Let's start over.' And we did."

She folded her hands and made a triangle with her thumbs.

"I don't think you get to pick who your soul mate turns out to be. I was in love with your daddy," Mama went on. "But the person who knew me best—without glamour, without sparkle, who saw the best in me despite myself—that was Lenore. She loved us, you and me."

"She died when she gave birth to me," I said, though it made me afraid to say it.

Mama waited a while, and then just said simply, "Yes she did."

"When do you go back to Canaan?" I asked after a moment. I didn't notice until after I said it that I hadn't said we.

Mama swallowed. "Well, this is the big news I'm nervous to tell you." She paused, then began again with difficulty. "I kept the house and twenty acres for us, if we want to go back. The rest . . ." She looked at me. "I've sold to the Resettlement people, to replant. I was in the paper," she went on sheepishly. "I brought the clipping."

She showed it to me, a wrinkled square of paper she pulled from her bag.

"It says here Beezie and I are dead," I pointed out, amused.

Mama looked apologetic. "I told the reporter you were gone because of dust pneumonia. I think he thought I meant you were *gone.* People came out of the woodwork to offer condolences, and I had to explain over and over that it wasn't true."

I reread the article. Twenty acres was still a farm and a home. But I had a strange, sad, weightless feeling.

"What are we going to do with the money?"

She looked at me searchingly. "I used twenty-five dollars to get here. The rest, we have to decide."

I tried to think of what I wanted to say, but Mama went on.

"Do you *want* to go back home?" she asked.

"I don't know," I said.

"Neither do I," she said. "Even if there ends up being something to go back to, I really don't know at all." She looked at me. "Maybe it's not too late for me to be someone who is brave."

This brings me to my second big news, Ellis. And what is hardest to say.

A few days after Mama and I talked, Sofia and I took our usual walk. Beezie pinged around us this way and that as we made our way to the river (now that she's well she is uncontrollable, a bolt of lightning ricocheting off the walls).

We walked past fruit sellers and stands hawking meat and

flour, watching the seagulls over the water and the boats float past.

I'd never felt, that day, less like I belonged anywhere at all: no longer sure about going home, but not at home in the city either. On the edge of something even more unknown than leaving Canaan.

Sofia and I leaned on a railing to watch the boats. Manhattan can be beautiful, Ellis, if you are willing to see it and not compare it to what you loved before.

She turned to look at me. "I'm getting so many customers at the stables. I think they'd follow me if I left. So I'm thinking of starting my own," she said. "I already found a space to rent, and I just have to put down a deposit."

I listened, thinking how brave she was to try.

"I was thinking . . . there will be too much work for just me."

"You're offering me a job?" I asked, surprised. I felt, at that moment, as if the dust had jumped from Beezie's lungs to mine, and my chest squeezed. I guess this is the way some moments that decide our future happen; with a few little words on a walk.

"It's not much, it's not our dream, but we could make the best of things here. You and Beezie and your mother could get your own place, and I could too. We could be those people who can afford a taxi someday," she teased, and then turned serious. "To be honest, I feel like, with Beezie here, it's like having a piece of my dad. I couldn't save him, but I helped to save her. And every time I look at her, it reminds me of that. It feels like I can say to him, 'Look, I'm doing things right.'"

Sofia watched me nervously. I think she could already see that I was going to say no, because she became more solemn as she looked at me.

I said finally, "I have a proposal too."

Not a day goes by when I don't see home in my mind. The pond and the garden, always faltering under our hands, and the dust whirls—when they were small—lifting across the Chiltons' fields and whirring toward us like ghosts. I even miss the sight of that, Ellis—can you believe it? How is it that home invades you like that? How can I ever get over the loss of it? Especially now, when it's slowly coming back to life and I'm not there to see it?

I know I'll miss it forever, but I also know that I can't give into that. As much as I've always loved Canaan and loved you, I want my life to go forward even if it hurts. And I've decided I have to reach for what I want even if my hands are trembling from fear. I'm sorry, Ellis, but I'm not coming home.

We've come halfway across the country and now we only have to get across the sea. Now that New York's gotten easier, I am leaving it for something I've only dreamt about. I want to soak the drizzly English rain into my skin and see green wherever I go, and visit the Cave of the Cup, and walk the paths Mama and Lenore used to walk. I want to see where they were born, and see what they saw.

We leave tomorrow. We've written to the Allstocks that

we're coming—well, and that I exist at all—and we hope they'll welcome us once we're there.

I'm not taking all that much with me. I have this journal, and Beezie and Mama, a few clothes, and a photo of Mama and Lenore she gave to me the other night. They're holding each other's waists; Lenore is pregnant enough to pop. But they look so happy, hugging for dear life.

Mama says God will show us the way forward. Her faith never changes, while mine does all the time—blinking out at times, flaring up at others. For the moment, I think maybe there *is* a God but a different one than she says. I think God might be the dust and the jackrabbits and the rain, that God might be Teddy and the bullet that killed him, the beautiful and exquisite moon and the terrible zeppelins, all spread out and everywhere. I've begun to think that maybe we are God's fingers rubbing against each other to see how it feels. Do you think that is a sacrilegious thought—that God might be everything and its opposite?

A farm is a very small thing to offer in return for a sister's life. But it's all I have to give. I've told Sofia what's left of our land is hers . . . if she can bring herself to leave the city and take another big chance. I know it's just a dried-up piece of nothing for now. But I think someone like her, with everything she knows and everything she'd be willing to give, might be able to pull it back from the brink. I want the farm to stay in our family if I can, and that's what Sofia is now. It belongs to her already, I think, according to something written under the surface of things that I can't claim to understand but only feel. I think she might even be a match for Galapagos.

Ellis, you once said you could save us, and I couldn't afford to believe it. As tempting as it is to pin myself to anyone else's strength—Mama's or Sofia's or yours—I have to navigate my life myself.

I don't think you *can* leave a person you love without leaving your skeleton behind. But I also think that sometimes you can't stay.

Mama said once that dreams can only keep their sparkle when they stay far away. It makes me think about her and Lenore and the Cave of the Cup and looking for things that may or may not exist. Maybe the important thing isn't the Grail, but that people looked for it in the first place.

I need to go out and see what I can see. I think the rest of the world is not as cold and lonely a place as you think. At least I have to hope.

I'm enclosing fifty dollars, to pay back what I owe you, plus inflation. It adds up to the cost of passage on a ship to Southampton, should you ever decide to use it. It's another of my far-fetched desires, I suppose, to think you might let me save you instead.

I hope you get this letter. I hope one day you change your mind and find your way to Forest Row. I hope you miss me still. I hope you'll meet me there.

Love, Catherine

ADRI

PART 3

CHAPTER 11

Lily and Adri sat on the couch, the pile of letters in Adri's lap. Adri had just finished reading them out loud to Lily while she fiddled with the buttons on her sweater and stared into the fire.

"Do you think he went after her?" Lily asked, as if it were a romance novel they'd just finished reading.

"I think he buried her letters in a wooden box and married Lyla Pearl," Adri said.

Lily looked at her, exasperated, her eyes filling with tears. "You have no soul," she said.

"I think he went after her," Adri said more seriously. "And left everything behind. I'd bet anything."

"I don't know," Lily said.

Adri leaned back, spent. "Catherine lived. She saved Beezie. That's enough for now. It's more than I hoped."

Lily tapped her nails together, turning serious.

"It's nice," Lily said. "To get these pieces of my mother—from when she was young. I always knew she was a firecracker." She paused. "But she wasn't related to them. I guess we're the last in the family after all."

"I hope you don't need any perfect match transplants anytime soon."

"Just the brain," Lily said.

Adri still felt the pinch of grief, but she wasn't disappointed. They were the last of a family line that had wound its way through a woman who cut her hair because it was in the way, and saved someone who'd needed saving, and brought a dead farm back to life.

It felt like a good history to own. Something to be proud of. And still it left something dangling—one piece still in need of tending to.

After a while, she said, "I think there's something I want to ask Lamont for. But it's really up to you."

The aircraft they were to fly in, Lamont had said, would be a small Hover Freight, the size of a van. A biologist would come to meet them.

Lily kept swiveling around in the passenger seat the whole way to the airport, talking to Galapagos, whom they'd loaded into the folded-down back seat using a dolly and some ropes.

"I think she's carsick," she kept saying, but Galapagos's face in Adri's rearview mirror was the same as it always was—a little disapproving and a little curious. She did appear to be looking out the window.

The Hover Freight, the pilot, and the scientist who had come to meet them—Trevor—were already there when they arrived.

"It's an honor to meet you, Adri," he shouted as the pilot helped her and Lily on board, and two others lowered a stretcher to lift Galapagos.

"Thank you for doing this," Adri said, shaking his hand before taking a seat beside him.

"We're thrilled to have her," Trevor said.

Lily, in the seat ahead of them, looked around the cabin, nervous. "Well put flying on this thing on the list of stuff I could have died happily without ever doing," she said.

She gasped as they lifted off and pressed her hands to the window.

"It's laying season right now," Trevor explained, "so we're very selective about when and how we come in and out. We like to give the animals their peace. This girl," he nodded toward the back of the compartment, where Galapagos lay strapped to a pallet, hissing at them, "will be happy there, I think."

In no time they were crossing the crisp line of the coast below, and then they were out over open water. It only took five hours to reach the crystal-blue water of the Eastern Pacific and for the Galapagos Islands to come into view—green grassy humps of land rising out from the water, verdant and pristine, no signs of human life anywhere in sight.

"It looks like mold," Lily said. "But pretty."

Adri surveyed the unspoiled landscape, the exotic, unimaginable beauty of it, and tried to picture James's parents arriving here all those years ago. After sailing for months, it must have looked to them like they'd reached a paradise at the edge of the world.

"We've built a living barrier around the perimeter. We're trying to keep it protected, along with its inhabitants. We'll be checking in on her regularly," Trevor said. "We'll give her any help she'll need to transition—food as she learns to forage on her own, things like that. We have a fair amount of experience rewilding tortoises that have been domesticated."

They landed quietly on a beach, in a puff of white sand. "We can't stay long," their guide said. "We can't disturb the laying mothers."

Their helpers lowered the stretcher out of the back and carried it about a hundred yards down the beach, to a rolling dune that looked down on a gathering of tortoises, digging in the sand to lay eggs. Galapagos hissed as she was lowered onto the ground and released from the latex belt. She looked around at everything, and Adri tried to read her: was she scared? Did she remember the smell of the ocean?

They slid her off the stretcher onto the sand.

Everyone stood back but Lily, who stepped closer and knelt, with some effort, in the sand.

"Hey, old friend, do you remember the wild?" she asked. Galapagos just stared around. "Do you remember this is where you belong?"

"Would you like a minute alone?" Trevor asked.

Lily looked uncertain, like she was breaking a rule. "If I could . . . ," she said.

"Of course."

At first Adri thought it would be the three of them left alone, but then, looking at Lily, she realized she, too, was expected to back away. She walked back to the Hover Freight, and while the guys climbed inside, Adri stood and leaned against a rock, watching Lily and Galapagos in the distance.

Lily was rubbing the tortoise's head and talking to her.

Finally, she stood, dusted off her knees, wiped at her face, and walked toward them.

Their eyes traveled to Galapagos, still poised on her dune, not moving yet, just looking around, like she'd landed on an alien world.

They climbed into the aircraft, Adri helping Lily and then climbing in herself.

Nobody spoke as they lifted off; there was no small talk like there had been flying in. Their companions seemed to realize what the moment meant to them.

"What did you say?" Adri asked. "Do you mind if I ask?"

Lily smiled though tears were running over the corners of her lips. "I said, 'Be brave. The other tortoises aren't that bad.'" She paused to breathe, and gazed out the window, not meeting

Adri's eyes. "I told her, 'You'll realize how to be free if you just give it a little while. It can hurt a little bit, but that doesn't mean it isn't right. I'll be praying for you. I love you.'" Lily sniffed. "'You're my best friend.'"

Adri didn't trust herself to say anything for a while. "That's good," she said after a few moments. "You said the right things."

At first they could see the tortoise—the shape of her, her lopsidedly round outline in the sand, her neck craned in curiosity. Not looking in their direction but away, out toward the rest of the island. And then she was a dot, and then—as the island retreated into the shape of green curves on the water—they couldn't make her out at all, and Adri could only picture her and what she wanted for her—that she would make her goofy, lopsided way down the dune toward the others. That she would remember she was home after all. That it would all come back to her.

On their drive back from Wichita, Lily insisted on listening to the entire collection of Phil Collins's greatest hits.

"This is my soundtrack for when I feel melancholy," she said.

"Well it's awful," Adri said.

"That's only because you have no soul," Lily said.

Adri shrugged. "Maybe you're right."

"I need to know you're going to be all right," Lily said abruptly.

Adri shook her head. "I need to know that about *you*."

Lily looked over at her. "Oh, Adri, I'll be fine." She glanced up at the sky. "My angels are looking after me."

"You don't know that."

Lily shrugged. "You don't know they're not."

There was nothing more to say about it. Nobody knew anything for sure.

"It's your last night," Lily offered. "What do you want to do?"

"Watch TV, I guess," Adri said.

Lily cooked her a pitiful dinner—spaghetti and jarred sauce. They watched *Bot Wars*, where people repurposed old androids and fought them in glow-in-the-dark arenas. "This is trash," Lily said, popping popcorn in her mouth. And at eleven, they went to bed.

It was like any other night, but it was the last night.

The darkness had fallen fast, and Adri kept looking up at the moon through the window. She thought about how almost everyone who came and went on Earth from the cavemen on had touched their eyes on the moon, but only a few people had ever been lucky enough to make their way past it. And she was going to be one of them. And that felt like breaking away from something in good and bad ways.

One last time, she read Lenore and Catherine's letters. And then she went to sleep that night using her old positive visualization trick, but this time she visualized something she knew for sure could never happen. She saw Lily walking to the edge of the farm and finding a cave. In it was a Cup that made you live forever. In her vision, her cousin drank from it, and did.

CHAPTER 12

It was an hour's drive to the launch site. Adri watched the farm disappear behind her, then Jericho Road, then, as they entered the highway, Canaan. She and Lily didn't speak the whole way. She'd brushed her hair for once, and now she ran her hands through it.

She clutched a letter in her one less-than-twenty-pounds bag and everything it contained.

They exited at Garden Plain and, after parking, got out of the car without exchanging a word.

A scattering of journalists waited for them, calling Adri's name as they got out of the car. A few cameras flashed; a reporter called out, "Good luck!" Lily gave a friendly wave and followed Adri up the gangway into the building. Families had come into town for good-byes, and the vestibule was crowded.

They were separated while Adri suited up and while the last tests were being performed. The others all gathered around their locker pods, but everyone was quiet, in their own heads, and only vaguely acknowledged one another. Adri could hear the roar of the shuttle outside the building, hear people announcing the results of different diagnostic tests over loudspeakers.

She felt suddenly, terrifyingly breakable. What if their ship exploded before it even got there? Why had she never thought to worry about that? What if it caught fire the moment they took off? She thought of all the things she'd forgotten to be scared of.

She looked over to see Saba's hands trembling a little on her locker as she closed it.

"We'll be fine," Adri said. "If you want to vomit on someone, you can vomit on me."

Outside, in a room that gave way to the hallway that led to the ship, Lily stood among the other families, tiny compared to everyone else, her white hair and pale face standing out in the crowd. She looked like a little kid on the first day of school—excited, proud, scared, lost.

"Are you ready?" Lily asked, as they lingered at the edge of the crowd. People around them were saying their good-byes, hugging, crying. Adri's heart began to pound out of her chest.

"I guess," Adri said. "I guess this is what feeling ready feels like." She swallowed. "Any advice?"

Lily's face crumpled up and tears ran down her cheeks. She took Adri's hands in hers and squeezed them hard, hers were small and thin. "Enjoy yourself," she said.

They stared at each other. So many thoughts were running through Adri's head, but there would never be enough time to say them all. And because she couldn't say all of them, she didn't say any of them. She reached down into her bag and pulled out an envelope, handing it to Lily.

"Read it after I take off," she said.

Lily nodded.

Now people were starting to trail down the hallway, and a technician took Adri's bag and told her it was time to board. Adri couldn't bring herself to let go of Lily's hands. She held her hand to Lily's cheek before letting it drop.

She backed toward the hallway. And softly, the moment faded away. She let go.

The simulations couldn't have prepared her for what it was like looking out a window of a ship that was already far from Earth. The contrast of Adri's small warm bunk, her blankets around her that night . . . and what lay beyond the glass: the immensity of space, the hazy blue planet she was leaving, suddenly small and far away. It was like looking out at a rainstorm from a warm, dry house, and thinking of everyone else outside, exposed to the sky.

That night, the ship was quiet, everyone deep in their own thoughts. Adri watched the Earth spin behind them in its restlessness and thought about the future. Mars would have a history one day too, and she would be a part of it. It might be just the beginning—using Mars as a launch point, they might find life everywhere, scattered throughout the universe, pulsing and humming and wanting, inevitable, instead of just a fluke like so many believed.

If that was true, she hoped she lived long enough to find out.

CHAPTER 13

Lily got home late, long after dark. She'd stayed to watch the launch and then stayed with the other parents and friends to stare up at nothing for a while and listen to the echo of the coordinates being read off by someone on the ground crew. By now, she knew the ascent would be over and the shuttle would be in temporary orbit—she'd read about it in some literature the families had received.

The house was quiet. But also full. She guessed that was why people had housewarmings. Adri had warmed her house.

She put off opening the letter until after she'd put on her pajamas and climbed into bed. She tried to read a chapter of her latest romance novel, *Hearts on Fire*, to put it off. She wanted to savor this time when Adri still had something to say to her. But she couldn't concentrate, and finally she put down the book and picked up the envelope, tearing it open slowly.

Lily,

I'm writing this as fast as I can. I'm not much on writing, and I always wondered why some people are so drawn to it. But now as I sit here trying to think of what to say, I think I understand. No one wants to disappear. Words made things real, and they last so much longer than we do.

So, for the record, here are the things that I want to be real. And I hope that words are enough to make them that way:

One: Lenore Allstock dies in childbirth but wakes up in heaven, surrounded by angels.

Two: Ellis Parrish tries to bury his memories of Catherine Godspeed in his bunkhouse floor, but time proves love can't be buried. He sails to England. He follows her.

Three: You are happy and safe, always.

Four: Everyone in the world is happy and safe, always.

Five: We get to Mars safely. We make something new, and we do it right. We pay attention.

I love you, Lily. I wanted to tell you most of all that I think it's our love that gets passed along.

Onward and forward.

Love, Adri

P.S. You told me to take all the letters with me. But I want you to have this one. It's just a postscript from Lenore. But it's my favorite.

JUNE 24, 1920

Dear Beth,

We're almost to New York, and I'll have to give you this letter in person. But I wanted to write it anyway.

I've been looking in the mirror a lot recently. I can't really picture what my face looks like to other people anymore. Every time I look I see someone different: sometimes young, sometimes old, sometimes wise, sometimes not. What will you see when you see me again?

So close to arrival, and I keep asking myself, since I have so much time to think, where did we lose each other? Was it when you left for America, in those weeks after the first zeppelin came? Or was it when I didn't get on that ship? Or does it go farther back? Was it when you took me looking for the Cup and told me where it was even though it wasn't true? Was it when you told me I couldn't run as fast as you, so I shouldn't even try?

I've decided that it doesn't matter, because it's not true. I haven't lost you, and you haven't lost me. I don't care if there are cracks in us, we are still us. We don't have to be perfect to be right.

The baby is on my mind all the time, even when I sleep. I am sure she is a girl, for no reason I can explain, and it suddenly seems to me that even the idea of babies is exquisitely, blindingly beautiful. How they arrive knowing nothing at all—what year they live in or where they live or that money exists or what Earth even is. My baby doesn't know yet that she's even on a planet at all; she doesn't know about the sun or that hordes of people can be terrible to each other. I think it's this innocence that is suddenly so shattering to me. I realize how the world doesn't seem to deserve this innocence. But we'll try to earn it, won't we, Beth?

I think now how strange it is that time moves at all. How logical it would be for nothing to ever change. Do you even remember me like I remember you? Am I keeping a dream alive that's only a childish memory? Do we know each other anymore, my friend? It doesn't matter. We are connected, you and me. The baby makes me realize that. The separations aren't real.

When James and I were together that last night, and he had his new torch, he said that for once, instead of looking at the stars, the spotlight would be on us. He turned it on and it flickered into bright-white light—putting a glow on our faces and casting a glow around our humble and beloved little room. It lit up his face and mine.

I was so nervous when I put my hand on his cheek and felt the scars and said, "You're a beautiful sight," and put my lips to his.

It's shocking, isn't it, that a kiss could have led to something so big and violent and full of light as a human being? It makes me dizzy just to think of all the things that start that way. Whole families, whole countries, whole worlds. Isn't it strange how a whole life can begin with a little spark?

I'll send you a postcard when I arrive in New York.

Love, Lenore

ACKNOWLEDGMENTS

Thank you to Mark for everything he does all the time . . . but especially for being my brave and honest first reader. Thank you to my sweet Owen for being such a good sleeper.

I'm deeply grateful to my editor, Jen Klonsky, and my agent, Rosemary Stimola, for their trust, talent, thoughtful feedback, and generosity. I'm also indebted to my friends and teachers at Bennington College and, in the case of this story, to Joanne Proulx in particular.

Jamie Appel gave me the gift of time by loving and caring for my son while I worked; I can't thank her enough. I also owe thanks to Alejandra Oliva, my acute and gracious sensitivity reader; Gareth Wade, my treasured pal and British test reader; to Jill Amack for her thoughtful eye; and to Becky Goldenbaum, whose faith inspired this book in ways I haven't yet expressed to her. Thank you always to my family.

These books informed my writing:

The Worst Hard Time by Timothy Egan

Great Britain's Great War by Jeremy Paxman

Elon Musk: Tesla, Space X, and the Quest for a Fantastic Future by Ashlee Vance

The Case for Mars by Robert Zubrin

An Optimist's Tour of the Future by Mark Stevenson